THE Bracelet

A time and place where two worlds collide

by

Jaren L. Davis

LIMITED EDITION

Limited Edition of *The Bracelet*, Sheridan Publishing, 2010

Printed in the United States of America
ISBN: 978-0-9727200-7-6

Thanks, Mom and Dad (my guardian angel),
for giving me life and starting me on my journey.
Kim, you are my strength and my foundation.
I am who I am because of you.
Jake, Katie, Sallie, and Lindie—whatever I did
to earn the right to be your father, I am grateful for.
Each of you are special and will accomplish much.
Nick Galieti, this story would have remained on my
computer without your suggestion of publishing.
Dan Hogan, we are kindred spirits. Thank you for
being inspired and for your extraordinary talent.
Last, thank you all who have been, are,
and yet will be a part of my life.
Enjoy this story—it has come from my heart.

Introduction

4:32 p.m. That's when Jim first noticed that nine-year-old Alice was missing.

The tour had been one of the most incredible experiences they had ever had as a family, but right now it was the furthest thing from Jim's mind. Alice was not to be seen, and the scare they had had last evening was still painfully fresh.

"Karen!" he whispered nervously. "Where's Alice?"

"She was over by that piece of statuary just a minute ago, Jim. She was with Lucy and Rick. I'm sure she's close. Ah, see, here come Lucy and Rick now," Karen assured as Rick came around a corner, his striking seventeen-year-old sister in tow.

"Rick, where's Alice? Mom said she was with you."

"Nope—must be with Johanna. We just stopped to look at the elephant painting again. Lucy just can't get over how cute it looks!" he mocked as he smiled at his younger sister.

"Not with me!" Johanna piped up as she stepped out from behind her mother.

"Jim?" Karen's motherly instincts kicked in. Turning to the children she demanded, "When was the last time any of you saw Alice?"

And that's when Jim first felt the magic of the place that was to enter their lives, for although he could hear their three older children stammer in self-defense, a calm unlike anything he had ever felt before enveloped him, not unlike the robes worn by the monks that still inhabited Angkor Wat—comfortable, warm, and just a little mysterious.

Without saying a word, Jim reached over and took his wife's hand, motioning with a nod of his head to follow. Though he had no idea where he was going, he knew exactly where they were headed. They were going to find Alice.

Jim and Karen quickly retraced their steps about 30 feet back down the hall, then felt drawn to turn right, even though they had come from the left. There, 15 feet away and chatting with an older man was little Alice, as comfortable as young Jesus must have been with the learned men on the steps of the Jerusalem Temple. Though the Callisters had never seen this man before, they both felt immediately that she was in no danger; in silence they stood back and watched the scene before them.

The older man was not kneeling in a western position but rather squatted comfortably as he gazed eye to eye with their daughter. Extracting something from a pocket in his robes, he pressed it into her hands, whispering warmly as he did so. Karen could not resist and raised her camera to capture the moment. An unusual feeling of gratitude washed over her just as she pressed the button— warm light from the late afternoon sun flooded her subjects through a lower window as her viewfinder revealed an image normally reserved for the front cover of *National Geographic.* With or without the picture, Jim and Karen would never forget that moment.

The flash seemed to alert the old man that he had visitors. He looked over at Karen and Jim—and their children, who had caught up to them and had been equally captivated by the scene—and immediately recognized the situation. A concerned family had come looking for their precious missing one. He smiled warmly at the little troupe, and they knew that Alice had been in no danger. Then turning back to Alice, he clasped her little hands in his own, tapped at whatever he had given her, and whispered gently. At that, he rose and shuffled off down the hall.

"Alice, who was that?" Johanna blurted out, now that the magic of the moment had gone with the disappearance of the old man. "What did he give you?"

"And why didn't you tell us where you were?" chastised the ever-protective Rick.

Alice gave her family the look that all nine-year-old girls seem to know instinctively, the one that says, *I knew exactly where I was this whole time. Don't get all huffy! There was nothing to worry about!* Walking up to her mother, she opened up her hand and said, "He gave me this bracelet. Isn't it pretty?"

Karen looked at the gift with a practiced eye—and was nearly mesmerized. It was simultaneously simple and elegant, bearing no precious stones yet somehow invaluable. Light blue stones were bound loosely together on a leather string—it reminded Karen of the old man himself: a simple exterior that belied the power that surged just under the surface. She reached out to finger the stones and sensed a warmth and peace deep in her heart as she did so. There was definitely something magical about this sacred temple!

Jim heard a step behind him and turned to see that Tree had joined them. "Did you see this older man, Tree? Do you know him?"

"I am sorry, Mr. Callister. I have never seen him before, although he walks as if he is comfortable with these surroundings. If that is the case, it is strange, for I give tours here regularly, and yet I have never seen him."

"His robes—they did not seem to be the same as the robes of other monks we have seen today. Do they mean anything to you?"

"Again I am sorry, Mr. Callister. They were unlike anything worn by our local monks, and yet I must admit that there was something hauntingly familiar about them, as if I should know them by sight and know of their considerable meaning. Very strange, I must say.

"One more thing that you should know, Mr. Callister. I overheard just a bit of what he was whispering to your little one. He was speaking a blessing, the words of which are very ancient and very sacred. Few outside this temple know this blessing. I only came across it last fall as I was browsing the archives looking for descriptions of how the temple was built. I found an old but very well preserved text that spoke of an unusual spirit that attended this most famous of all temples, a spirit that connected this world with the world of those who had passed on before. The bracelet that he gave your daughter contains very old symbols that remind one of this blessing and its meaning."

Though much of what the guide had said escaped Alice's understanding, she understood enough to know that this was a very unusual gift. But then, that was something that she already grasped as soon as the old man had wrapped his worn fingers around her young ones and pressed the bracelet tight against the palm of her right hand. As she looked up into her mother's deep blue eyes, she smiled, then radiated the afternoon light in her smile. Somehow they both knew that she would never be the same after this day.

Part One: The Journey

Chapter 1

Jim Callister was one of the lucky ones. Five feet ten inches tall with sandy red hair and what could be best describe as alert blue eyes, he was naturally strong. His years of competitive swimming had produced broad shoulders and a certain spring to his step that came from leaning over a pool for hours on end while practicing leaping as far as possible. Gifted with natural gregariousness and the ability to sell snow to an Eskimo, he was also an uncommonly good listener and built immediate trust with whomever he was speaking.

But if you were to ask anyone who knew Jim, you would learn that was not why he was considered one of the lucky ones. For that you had to look just slightly beyond him to the woman at his side. Jim Callister had married a stunning woman whom he met in his third year of college and fell absolutely head over hills in love with. They in turn had four great kids: Rick, Lucy, Johanna, and Alice. Jim had a good job, Karen was a wonderful mother, and life was going precisely according to their plans.

Until about six months ago. That's when the world turned on its side for the Callisters, and their perspectives changed in very significant ways.

Everyone loved . . . no, everyone absolutely adored Karen. What wasn't to adore? Five feet six inches of stunning beauty, rich green eyes, well read, outgoing—Karen was simply one of those individuals whom people were instinctively drawn to because they knew she could do anything she put her mind to. And chances are, they could too—as long as she was close by!

The oldest of six children, Karen had grown up being relied on to help as assistant mother to her younger siblings. She was also right-hand man to her father's part-time passion for farming. From both her parents, she learned hard work and independence, but she also learned the value of teamwork, especially as a family. Life was simply not manageable without the cooperation and assistance of everyone in the home, and Karen learned early the skill of peacemaking. It was a matter of survival, but it was also a gift that she sought and seemed particularly well suited for.

But as remarkable as Karen was, she could not stop the natural course of mortality. Oh, she tried. God knows how she tried! And so does everyone else who knows her. Perhaps more than anyone, Karen's next-younger sister Anne understood how much she wanted to change the course of life and time, for Anne was the subject of Karen's sacrifice.

The call had caught Karen in the middle of getting the kids ready for Saturday morning soccer. Rushing about with three pair of socks in one hand, a single shoe in the other, and a needle for pumping up flat balls clenched between her teeth, she had snatched the phone from its cradle on the third ring, just before it would have rolled over to the answering machine. Glancing quickly at the caller ID, she saw it was her closest sister, the one with whom she had shared a bedroom—and perhaps more importantly, a bathroom—for years. "Anne! How are you? I might need to call you back in a few—last minute soccer madness, you know."

A muffled half-sob slipped through the chaos around her and into Karen's ear.

"Anne? Never mind what I just said. I'm here for you. What's up, munchkin?"

Motioning to Jim, she dropped the socks, shoe, and needle into his lap, whispered *Something's wrong with Anne—you're on your own this morning!* and slipped into their bedroom, closing the door behind her. This was clearly not just a social call.

Subdued but now more controlled, Anne's voice came through, "Karen? Listen, I can call back later."

"Jim's got the kids covered. It'll be good for him to solo with the crew this morning—keeps him humble. It's just you and me, Anne. Tell me what's happened . . ."

"Cancer, that's what's happened. I just found out this morning, and I'm scared, Karen! This stuff happens to the woman down the street, or to your neighbor's sister—not to me! Megan's just turned one, Steve is still in school, and I've got cancer. Karen, why me? What am I going to do?"

And that was how Karen learned that her sister and her best friend outside of marriage, her little Anne, had been diagnosed with stage 3 bone cancer. The next day Karen was on the plane to Phoenix, where Anne, Steve, and little Megan had just purchased a two-bedroom condominium on the outskirts of Phoenix. Two weeks later, she found that her bone marrow was a good match for Anne, and three days after that she was in the operating room herself.

Nothing, not even child birth, had prepared her for the process of bone marrow donation. The injections that stimulated her marrow growth in preparation for surgery caused her joints to swell unmercifully. Everything ached as the centers for large bone mass in her body increased in growth five times. The constant pain at that depth of her physical body gave her a small appreciation for what her sister was going through.

Sadly, within weeks, Karen stood in the cemetery and watched her sister's casket lowered into the ground. She resolved to never leave anything undone that she felt she should do.

But apparently the Fates were not done tampering with the Callisters' lives. Just one week after Anne's funeral, Jim was hastened to the hospital. His father, the man who had not only helped rear him as a child but also had mentored his entrance into the brokerage business and had served as his partner during the early years, was finally succumbing to a chronic heart problem.

Frequently Jim longed for the day when people would talk about him as they did his father. Brent Callister was well known for his code of honor and for treating his follow workers with respect.

One evening Jim sat at his bedside and listened to his increasingly reflective father talk about his life. "Dad, I wish I felt as calm about all this as you do. Death doesn't seem to worry you nearly as much as some of the business deals we've worked through. I thought at first you were just trying to protect us from fearing the unknown, but as I've watched and listened to you, I think you're genuinely not afraid. What's up with that? You understand that this is not just another business trip that you're facing, don't you? You're not going to be coming home from this one."

"Listen, my boy. I don't think I have much time left now. I have lived a life that many people only dream of. I have everything I want, my children enjoy success and independence, and I'm feeling like I have walked on the trail of life until I have reached the summit. These past few days have given me a chance to turn around and see what I have accomplished. I am proud, I am content, and I'm a bit tired. Now let me take the next step."

Right then, right there, Jim realized the value of finding your passion, of not sweating the small stuff. Four days later, they buried Brent Callister, the finest man Jim had ever known. But with that burial, Jim experienced an awakening that, coupled with Karen's new resolve, would change their family in ways they could never imagine.

Chapter 2

"Jim, remember how much fun we had camping in the Canadian Rockies when the kids were younger?" Karen seemed to be on the hunt for adventure again, and Jim knew it was time to speak softly and carry a major credit card.

"Sure do, babe. Rick had the girls so worried about Big Foot moving in to our tent while we were hiking during the day that I thought they'd never set foot in a tent ever again."

"Oh, yeah, nearly forgot about that one. Do you know what I remember best about that trip?"

"Not a clue—what was it, Karen?"

"I think it was the exposure to a completely different environment. No running water, no curling irons, no electricity, just hiking up that trail each day and helping to clean it up for the Forest Service. I know it was only for three days, but I think it was good for the kids to see that we could survive for three days without texting or the Internet."

"Okay, I see where you're going. Then how about when we spent a week in Paris. We did the Louvre, the Eiffel Tower, that cool little cheese place, the historic cathedral tour. That was a real cultural eye-opener!"

"Well, yes, I suppose so. But, Jim, we stayed in air conditioned hotels and ate at decent restaurants every day. Was it really all that different?"

"Okay, then, how about the ranch in Wyoming summer before last? Living in a bunkhouse, riding horses, and eating dutch oven cooking—I don't remember any electricity there. At least not much."

"Oh, I don't know. Part of it is the primitiveness, but we did something more in Canada. We also spent most of our time providing service. Maybe that's what I'm looking for, Jim. All I know is that even though we've had some fantastic vacations as a family, sometimes I come home and wonder if it was worth it. It's like, I just saw some of the most amazing scenery in the world, but what difference does it make? Do you know what I mean?"

Jim raised his eyebrows, pursed his lips in thought, and went silent.

Karen waited a minute, then continued. "We have so much, honey. It amazes me how often we take little things for granted at home. Think of some of the simple pleasures—not just knowing the lights will come on when we flip the switch but also having stores with shelves filled with a variety of choices and knowing there is law and order with a choice of who leads us.

"There's something else that's been on my mind. I just can't shake it. You know as well as I know that experience is the best teacher sometimes. I had my work with my dad on the farm and helping Mom with all the kids; you had all your dedication to swimming and being the best possible athlete. And these kids of ours—we've worked so hard to make sure that they experience a lot of things in this world. But they're still middle-class American kids. That's all they know, Jim, and that's not enough."

Jim knew his wife well enough to know that his best course was to just listen—and admire. This was quite a woman, and when she got warmed up to an idea, he always benefited from paying attention to her.

"The more I think about this family, the more I'm convinced that becoming familiar with others' circumstances and understanding through experience that not everyone has the same opportunities that they have would prove to be an invaluable life lesson. I mean, when the kids have to give a report about a foreign country in school, they do a good job of learning about that country and giving a good report. But what do they really know about life in that country, Jim? How can they know what it feels like to grow up so poor that there is never enough food to eat or clean clothes to wear? I am absolutely persuaded that if we can provide them with a firsthand experience with the world, they will not only be more compassionate, but they will not take for granted the opportunities extended to them here at home. We just need to find the right place and the right experience."

"Karen, I can tell that you have thought a lot about this. You know that I trust your instincts. We have great kids with extraordinary talents, but maybe you're right. Maybe we need to push them—and us—outside of our comfort zones—way outside—in order to understand what they can really do to change their world. So, what do you have in mind?"

"I don't know yet. But I have a feeling that some very interesting doors are going to be opening for the Callisters soon. We just need to be ready."

Chapter 3

"Condoleezza Rice? *The* Condoleezza Rice? Don't be messin' with me now, John!"

"I knew you'd love to come with me to listen to her speak. Just be in the lobby of the Little America hotel tomorrow afternoon at 3:00, bone up on your current events a bit so you don't embarrass me, and we'll call my college debt to you finally covered. Fair?"

Jim hemmed and hawed a bit to tease his old friend. "I dunno, John. I mean, we've got to figure in the interest, compounded monthly of course, and then there was the inconvenience tax, and the finder's fee, and—"

"Don't push it, buddy! It's not like you proposed for me or anything. I mean, you made one simple introduction, and then hold it over my head for the rest of our lives."

"Simple introduction? John, I ensured that the family line didn't end with your sorry self. If not for that 'simple introduction' as you call it, you would have never married Kate and cleaned yourself up for a real job and life as a mature adult. Face it, I own you! You'll be owing me for the next 20 years at least!"

"Okay, Jim, I give. But since I'll never be able to repay you, I believe I know someone else who can use this invitation more than you. Listen, sorry to bother you, buddy. Don't worry about tomorrow, and I'll give you a buzz next week sometime. Tell you how it went."

"John?"

"Yeah, Jim?"

"*The* Condoleezza Rice?"

"That's what I said."

"I'll see you at three." And with that Jim hung up, having gone through the script one more time that they had used at least once every three months since graduating from college together in Finance. Oh, the details always changed, but the basic script remained the same—two good friends bantering back and forth until one figured the game had gone long enough and gave in to what they both wanted anyway. *But Condoleezza Rice?* Jim thought to himself. *John's pulled off a home run this time!*

Later that evening, Jim rehearsed the whole thing to Karen. Of course, he embellished the story a little, adding the drama and intensity to it that Karen had come to expect from his stories. She knew him well enough to guess about where the truth was and where the theatrics ended and appreciated his need to entertain as much as his need to share information.

She also knew of his love for networking. For some people, meeting people of power was a necessary evil, a part of a job that usually meant sucking up to egotistical men who were themselves sucking up to more powerful men. But that was not the case with Jim at all. Jim was simply fascinated with people. Jim loved people. He made them feel good with his genuineness and ready smile. Networking for Jim was like ordering fries with his hamburger—it was just the natural thing to do.

"But Jim?"

"Yeah babe? What is it?"

"Brush up a bit on your current affairs so you don't embarrass John, would you?"

Chapter 4

Jim arrived in the lobby of the Little America hotel before his friend John. That was not unusual, and the pattern had never bothered either of them.

Jim had had a good morning. Taking the good-natured ribbing from both his friend and his wife seriously, he had cleared his schedule and spent the morning searching the Internet for the latest information on issues that interested him, of course, but also on issues that he was less keen on but knew that they were relevant to Secretary of State Rice's international activities. He was particularly impressed with her commitment to not only take a strong stance against terrorism but also to improve the cultures in which terrorists are spawned so they would no longer be a natural product of the local environment.

Jim was also a believer in the principle of providing a positive environment for tomorrow's leaders to find their roots and their directions. For Jim this started in the home, his own home, in fact. Although he was fairly certain that Ms. Rice wouldn't necessarily make that connection between them, and he didn't plan on bringing it up, the thought nonetheless gave him a certain feeling of comradery and empathy for the celebrated former Stanford professor.

"Hi, Jim!" The familiar voice shook him out of his personal reverie.

"John! Nice of you to show up, mate," Jim chided. Then, "Seriously, I'm so excited I can hardly stand it. Thanks for thinking of me and allowing me to tag along with you."

"Any idea where we go?"

"Yeah, I chatted with a couple of members of the hotel staff while I was waiting—"

"Now, there's a surprise!" John interrupted. "You talking with total strangers as if they were your best buddies!"

Jim ignored the jab and continued, "And they said it's in this conference room just down the hall, turn to the right, and it should be the third door on the inside of the hotel. I guess the inside conference rooms are easier to secure than the ones with windows to the outside. And get this—they also told me that the room is one of the smaller meeting rooms in the hotel. That means that this is a fairly exclusive event, and we're not likely to be just faceless bodies in a mob. I'm thinking we might even get to shake hands or ask a question of her. What do you think?"

John couldn't help but enjoy the excitement on his friend's face. Heck, he felt more than a little jazzed about the prospects himself. He appreciated social and professional networking as much as the next guy, and maybe more, so Jim's information came as very good news. "Let's go find our seats then, shall we?" And off they went down the hall.

Turning the corner to the right, they immediately knew they were getting close. The entire hall was blocked off by plain-clothes security. Everyone wanting to go down the hall was checked to see if their names were on the invitee list (thankfully John had seen to it that Jim had been added yesterday). They were also quickly wanded and checked out by bomb-sniffing guard dogs before being allowed on to the designated conference room. It was obvious that the other rooms on the hall were being left empty for security reasons.

At the door, their names were checked against the list again, and then they were shown to their assigned seats. The bell hop had been right—this was not a large room. Seating was restricted to about twenty people, and Jim recognized several of them. As soon as they were seated, he began making small talk with a couple of the people around him.

About seven or eight minutes later, a man in a well-fitted but not necessarily expensive dark gray suit opened the door and walked to the front of the room. "Ladies and gentlemen, I am absolutely delighted to welcome you today. It is a rare opportunity that we have today, so without standing on any further ceremony, let me introduce you to our current Secretary of State, Ms. Condoleezza Rice!"

Through the same back door, in walked the woman who was twice voted the most powerful woman in the world. Slender, self-assured, dressed in a two-piece black business dress suit with a rather attractive broach pinned to her left lapel, she stood 5'8" and walked with the confidence of someone who had nothing to prove and a great deal to share. When she reached the speaker's rostrum, she placed one hand lightly on the nearest corner and smiled. "Thank you so much for inviting me here today. It is a privilege for me to meet with people who form the backbone of this great nation and who have sufficient personal backbone to stand for what is right in our world today." With that, she was off on her message of the day.

Jim was fascinated as Condoleezza invited them into a portion of her world. She was frank, insightful, and surprisingly quick-witted, an attribute that she did not often allow herself to reveal in more formal settings. After about 50 minutes, she opened up the remaining time for questions. Jim waited patiently as some of the more politically aggressive people in the room raised their hands. Besides, they asked good questions, and he really wanted to hear her answers.

At last, the time seemed right. When there was a break in the action, Jim raised his hand: "Ms. Rice, my name is Jim Callister. Could you tell us something of the people of Iraq? How do they feel about the war, and is that significantly different from your own feelings?"

"Jim, that's a very good question. It is very unfortunate we as Americans, and they as Iraqis, have a perception of each other that is tainted by the stories in the media. If we could send our families to Iraq to live with their people, and if the Iraqis could send their families here to live with us in America, I believe we would have no differences. They are much as we are—family oriented, loving, kind, and willing to share. They are wonderful people; they just don't really know who we are."

That's pretty much what Karen has been telling me, Jim thought to himself. As Condoleezza moved on to the next question, Jim's mind wandered back to some of their recent discussions at home. *Well, this certainly validates Karen's desire to share the world, its people, and its experiences with their children. I can't wait to talk to her this evening at home.*

∞ ∞ ∞

Thus began Karen's search. Guided as much by instinct as

by the research she conducted, she began to spend hours surfing the Web and searching for service opportunities. Karen was truly surprised at the large numbers of organizations sponsoring projects. Three countries, however, fit both the criteria that Karen had established and the deep feelings that seemed to be stirring her heart—Brazil, China, and Cambodia.

Years later, Karen remembered with clarity turning the page on her calendar and marking the day when she sent off that final battery of e-mails requesting information. February 1. It was a Tuesday.

On February 10, Karen received her first response. She took that as a sign, as did the guiding angels that she felt attended this call to action. A humanitarian missionary named Mike Johnson from their home town was serving in Cambodia. Wow! Could this be the break she'd been looking for? Immediately she responded to Mike and asked for more information.

As Karen shared her findings with Jim, he saw it in her eyes, more clearly every day—the Callisters were headed to Cambodia. What adventures awaited them they could only imagine.

Actually, whatever they did imagine would turn out to be grossly inaccurate.

Chapter 5

"You're probably getting tired of hearing me say this, Jim, but I feel so strong about this whole thing. Everything is falling into place—my feeling about a service-oriented vacation, your meeting Condoleezza Rice, connecting with Mike in Cambodia, and now this! I think this will be good to get the perspective of someone who lived in Cambodia and still has family there."

"Yeah, I can't believe I'd forgotten about RP until the kids pulled out our high school yearbook last Monday night." Mostly the girls loved to look at the changes in fashion and hairstyles—and of course giggle mercilessly over how geeky everybody looked "in the olden days." But as they were looking at Jim's photo with his swim team—*state champion swim team!* Jim remembered proudly—Jim saw RP standing right in the middle of the front line. Of course he would be in the front—not because RP loved attention and being seen, for he was a bit shy by nature, but because he was the shortest and slightest of frame on the team. Placing him almost anywhere else meant he would simply not be seen, and not seeing RP was unthinkable. RP had been their fastest sprinter, swimming almost with an air of desperation that drove him to state record speeds.

Jim wasn't sure what the initials "RP" stood for. He thought he had seen his name once, but it was long and difficult to pronounce, let alone remember, so everyone just called the former refugee RP. He had escaped from Cambodia, his home country, when he was thirteen, swimming a treacherous river with his aunt. That's about all Jim could remember, but it was enough. When Karen had pointed to his picture and said, "Jim, who is this? I think you need to call him for some reason," Jim knew that another puzzle piece was finding its place.

Fortunately, between Google, Facebook, and Jim's natural social networking skills, finding him was not difficult. He still lived in town, and now they were meeting him for dinner at one of the swim team's old haunts—a little hole-in-the-wall place not far from the school that served the best mushroom burger to ever grace the planet.

"RP! You look just like you did in high school—in all the right ways!" Jim said as he greeted his old teammate. RP smiled back—still shy, reserved, and slight of build but smiling with unabashed pleasure at seeing his friend again. "Listen, this is my wife, Karen. Karen, meet RP, the fastest guy to ever swim in this state."

After introductions, they placed their orders, for old time's sake going with cheese fries, onion rings, and the sloppy mushroom burgers with which they had celebrated victories twenty years earlier. Normally, Karen would never have let Jim get away with such a meal, but this was a special occasion, and she wanted to ensure the two men were as comfortable with each other as possible. Besides, she had a feeling that they would face much more challenging food than this in the villages of Cambodia.

After the usual reminiscing about glory days gone by, Karen decided it was time to dive a little deeper. "RP, Jim told me that you escaped from Cambodia when you were younger. If you don't mind, could you tell us about that? That must have been difficult."

Karen saw a dark cloud pass quickly across RP's face, so quickly in fact that she wondered at first whether she had just imagined it. "Ah, yes, difficult is a good word, Mrs. Callister—"

"Please, it's just Karen," she interrupted.

"Yes, then Karen. I should start with a brief history lesson. In the mid-1970s, the Communist leader Pol Pot came to power with the movement you might know as the Khmer Rouge. My father was an accountant in Phnom Penh, but the Khmer Rouge was committed to agrarian communism and forced him to leave his job and become a farm laborer. The poor living conditions and regular political executions brought about the death of one of every five citizens of my country.

"Though the Vietnamese removed him from office in 1979, conditions did not improve much. Rather, most of the next decade saw much civil war. But before Pol Pot was brought down, my father was foraging for extra food in the forest and accidentally set off one of the many land mines that are buried throughout the country. Thousands are still there today, waiting for the unsuspecting animal or careless human to find them. Anyway, my father did not die, but his legs were damaged so badly that he could only shuffle along slowly. Life was very difficult. My father could work very little, I was the oldest son and did what I could, and my two sisters were younger than I. My mother worked from morning to night to provide what she could for us.

"In the spring of 1979, my Aunt Samnang came to my father—her brother—and told him that she was going to escape. She wanted no more of that lifestyle. She begged them to come with her—she said she would carry her brother all the way to America if he couldn't walk. But they knew it would be impossible, and their presence would very likely mean the failure of her escape attempt. Father could not walk, Mother would never leave him, and my sisters were too little. I was sixteen. In the end, they decided to send me, both as a help to Aunt Samnang and as a means of giving me a chance at a life they could never hope for themselves—a life of freedom and safety.

"I will not go into the details of our escape. I will say only, for Jim's interest, that it included swimming a very treacherous river. I do not know to this day how we survived it. I believe it required the work of an entire division of guardian angels, but eventually we made our way to a refugee camp in Vietnam. From there, we were fortunate to find passage with some American military men to the United States. One of them was from Utah, and he helped us begin our new lives. That is how I came to your high school. I swam on the team because it reminded me every day of God's mercy in allowing me to find freedom, and every time I competed, I imagined I was back in the river, swimming for my very life." Here he paused and smiled. "I guess it worked pretty good, huh?"

"And your family?" Karen asked softly.

"I have no word. For twenty-five years I have written letters and tried all I could to find them. Six times I have returned to Cambodia for five weeks each time. I can find nothing. But I remain hopeful. Something in my heart tells me that they live yet, though I do not know how or where."

"Perhaps we can help," Jim offered. "We hope to visit there this summer with our son and three daughters. In fact, that is the main reason I contacted you. We know very little about the country and hoped you could tell us more."

Again Karen perceived a cloud in RP's dark eyes. "Jim, Karen, I appreciate the offer to help me find my family, but you would be much wiser to stay home. Do not go to that country. It is my homeland, and I have deep feelings for it, but you should not go there. Not for me, not for you, not for any reason."

Jim exchanged a glance with his wife, then pursued RP's warning. "I know that you have lost much in Cambodia, RP. But I thought that it was much safer now to visit. The tourist industry is not large, perhaps, but it is growing, and relations with the world community seem to be improving."

"I do not wish to frighten you, Jim. Let me explain my warning. You said you have daughters. How old are they?"

"Lucy is seventeen, Johanna twelve, and our little Alice is nine. And we also have a son, Rick, who is nineteen—he's the oldest."

Glancing at Karen and flushing just a bit, RP continued, "And are they as beautiful as your wife? Please forgive me for being so bold, Karen."

"Oh, I don't mind the compliment at all, RP," Karen laughed.

And Jim added, "Actually, they are very much like their mother in that regard. I am, whether I like it or not, the thorn in the midst of four beautiful roses."

"And Rick's no slouch," Karen chipped in. "But why do you ask?"

"Cambodia is home to a flourishing and very well run slave trade. American girls bring a high price, and if they are attractive—such as your wife, Jim—they will bring top dollar."

"Slave trade?"

"Let me be blunt so you do not misunderstand, Jim, Karen. By slave trade, I mean sex slaves. Girls, including the age of your youngest, are stolen while on vacation in this foreign and interesting country, and sold to clients throughout Asia and Eastern Europe. They will be forced to take drugs until they are so dependent they cannot live without them; their sex masters keep them drugged enough that their senses are dulled but not so much that they can't perform what they are told.

"Please, if you love your girls at all, as I know you do, do not take them to Cambodia! The risk is just not worth it!"

Karen was speechless. How could anyone do such a thing to innocent young women? Surely RP was mistaken!

As if reading her mind, Jim asked, "How do you know of such things, my friend? You speak as if you know what you are talking about."

This time RP's eyes flashed with a strange mix of sadness and anger. "Although American girls bring the top dollar on the sex slave market, they are not the only ones victimized by these ruthless devils." He paused, then continued more subdued. "I left two young sisters behind. They are in my mind every day and every night. You must believe me when I say that I have searched everywhere for them. Understand? I know what I'm talking about. Do not take your daughters to Cambodia, Jim. If you do, you will regret it."

Jim and Karen drove home in silence, each deeply disturbed by what they had just heard. And that evening when they sent their children off to bed, Jim lingered a bit longer at each bedroom door, searching his heart for answers.

First was nineteen-year-old Rick, their only son and oldest of the children. Rick was built much like his father, only blond, and much more reserved. He had the heart of lion, but was one of the kindest, sweetest young men Jim knew. Because of his shyness, he was sometimes misperceived as being conceited. An unfair assessment, but life happens.

Lucy was seventeen and gorgeous, with long blonde hair and a smile to die for. Gregarious, a talented artist, and an independent woman prepared with her life plan. Her organizational skills provide comfort to all who are blessed to be with her.

Johanna was the athlete, a class officer, and had been asked to do some photo shoots by a local talent agency, but that was just not her thing. Though just twelve, she was already a much-watched swimmer by college scouts throughout the western states, and her reputation was still growing. Of all the girls, Johanna looked most like her mother, a fact that both Kim and Johanna were quite pleased with.

And finally, Jim paused especially long at Alice's door. She was but nine years old, but both Jim and Karen had noticed something special about Alice. Sure, she was a fine little gymnast and a lot of fun to be around, but Alice just seemed more connected with the universe around her. She had an unusual spiritual sensitivity and a moral maturity beyond her years. Besides that, she was their youngest, and what father's heart isn't deeply embedded in his baby's life.

Karen slept not at all that night, and it had nothing to do with cheese fries, deep fried onion rings, or the sloppiest mushroom burgers on the planet. Neither did it really have anything to do with whether the Callisters should continue their plans, for she was absolutely convinced that this was something her family must do. But no mother wants to place her children in danger, and RP's warning was anything but vague.

Chapter 6

A week after the dinner with RP, Karen was still in turmoil. Sleep, when it came, was marginal. *How can I protect our children, especially these precious, beautiful daughters?* she asked herself approximately six times a minute.

"Mom, do you ever dream that you're a superhero?" Johanna asked one morning at breakfast.

"No, not really, honey. I usually leave the superhero stuff to my daytime hours—comes with the job of being a mother."

"No, really, Mom. I had this really weird dream last night. The whole family was walking through this jungle, like we were going on a picnic or a treasure hunt or something. You were our guide, and you had like this superhero X-Ray vision so you could tell us which path to go down. And all around us were, like, lions and tigers and really creepy guys. We could hear them, but they couldn't come close because Dad and Rick had these force field suits on. Some bad dudes came down our path from the other direction, and they didn't even see us. Walked right past us, like we were invisible. And then we—"

"And then we came to a clearing, right?" Lucy interrupted. "With this humongous building in the middle? And all these guys with robes, like they wear in those corny kung fu movies that Dad likes to watch when he thinks no one is looking, except these were all good guys. You could tell."

"Yeah, but how did you know what was in my dream?"

"Same dream two nights ago. That's just way freaky—just like that *Medium* show on TV. Did we watch some Indiana Jones movie together or something? I don't remember it."

"I don't get it, Mom. How can we both have the same dream?"

"I don't know, honey, but I think I know what it means."

"What?"

"It means that tonight I'd better get some sleep. It takes a lot of energy to use super X-ray vision. And I think we're going to be just fine on our trip to Cambodia."

Chapter 7

The next four months flew by. Karen was in her element—focused on a worthy cause. Her journal was getting filled with uncanny experiences. Take her entry for March 12, for example:

Today we went to the post office to apply for passports for the kids. Things have changed since Jim and I got ours a couple of years ago. The lines were long and the recent terrorist threats both here in the U.S. and abroad have really done a number on the length of time required for processing. As a result, the clerks at the post office were cranky, the people in line were cranky, our kids were cranky, and the whole mess was just a bit tense. When we finally got to the front of the line, the clerk asked when we would be traveling and where we were going. When she learned our destination was Cambodia and we hoped to leave in 90 days, she just shook her head. "I don't know if you'll make it," she said. "You can try. Paying the express fee is more expensive, but you ought to consider it if you want to get there with your kids." So I paid the extra money. As I handed the woman the credit card, I felt like I should tell her more about our trip. I explained that we were going to do a family service project and that we were more interested in helping orphanages than lying on the beach. She was quite impressed and promised to call her cousin in the San Francisco processing office about our request—no promises, but she'd try to make sure that we received them in time.

On March 26, she wrote:

Our passports arrived in the mail for the kids today! I don't know how it happened when so many others are taking so long, but there is obviously a purpose for the Callisters to go to Cambodia!

April 3 brought this entry:

We got out second round of vaccination shots today. The children took it all in stride, challenging each other to be first and be the example for the rest. Poor Jim—he was white as a ghost. He just cannot handle getting stuck by a needle. I never worry about him becoming a junkie though—he doesn't have the stomach for it. To his credit, he took it like a man and got through the whole experience. He didn't squeal, scream like a little girl, or pass out. (Of course, I did have to drive us all home as he was still a bit out of sorts.) That's my man! Now just one more round to go...

My only moment of real concern today was when I saw the map of disease in third world countries. Cambodia was the front and center leader for malaria. It was a good reminder to trust my instincts and Jim and Rick's protective force fields!

But the most impressive of all her entries came just three weeks before they were to leave:

When I first heard from Mike in Cambodia several months ago, one of the things that touched me most was his comment about the need that their children's hospitals and orphanages alike had for blankets. These poor children were not only missing their families but also other basic needs, such as the ability to stay adequately warm when they were chilled from sickness. Sweets were unthinkable, every spare dollar that was available went to medicine and basic food stuff just to sustain life.

I mentioned their plight to my mother. You know how she is—the thought of one poor cold little girl was enough to motivate her into action. She just looked at me, patted me on the hand, and said, "Honey, don't you worry about a thing. I've got this under control." Occasionally she would remind me to not worry, and last night I found out why.

My dear mother had rallied her friends together, and they got in touch with their friends. Soon, whole neighborhoods pitched in. They made blankets, tied quilts, bought little stuffed animals, and purchased several large bags of suckers. It's a good thing that Jim is a master packer—that man can get more into a bag than Mary Poppins! And he'll need every inch of space to fit all this in. I'm so excited to see the faces of these sweet little children when we show them what we've brought!

Chapter 8

"Good morning, ladies and gentlemen, this is your captain. For those of you who were able to sleep, we hope that you have had a pleasant and restful flight over the last several hours. As you can probably feel, we have just begun our descent to the Phnom Penh airport. The temperature this morning is already a balmy 80 degrees and climbing.

"We are the only flight landing at the airport this morning, which puts us right at the front of the line. We are actually landing just a few minutes early, so our projected arrival time at the gate is right at 9:40 local time.

"It's been a pleasure to fly with you . . ." As the pilot ran through the usual well-rehearsed script, Jim leaned over his wife and looked out of the airplane window at the land below. It was just as RP had described for them. A rather large river meandered through the endless rice fields, and he wondered if that was the famous Mekong River that he had heard so much about.

"Hey, Mom?" Alice's voice drifted up from the seat behind.

"Yeah, honey. Did you get any sleep on the flight?"

"Did she ever!" chipped in Lucy. "She settled in on my shoulder and didn't move for about 83 hours! I don't think I'll ever be able to play the piano again!"

"I wouldn't worry too much, dear. I happen to know for a fact that there are some absolutely marvelous pieces written for one hand. You'll learn to deal with this new challenge."

"Hush for a minute, Lucy. I wasn't that bad! Anyway, Mom, are we getting close? I didn't understand what that man said. It was like talking to the thing at McDonald's when you drive through and order food from the car—wah, wah, wah, wah!"

"Yes, Alice, we're almost there. Make sure you keep your seat belt done up until we're safely on the ground. They'll tell us when we can unbuckle after we have landed."

Rick whistled softly. "Wow, this looks just like that documentary we had to watch in AP World History about Viet Nam. Just rice fields and jungle, and jungle and rice fields. The American soldiers had a really hard time adapting to this kind of country—and to the heat and humidity. I guess we'll find out about that in just a few minutes, eh?"

As the plane continued its descent, the city of Phnom Penh, Cambodia's capital, came into view. Jim could see well enough to see that the streets were mostly dirt, and they were laid out in no apparent order, at least compared to the orderly square blocks he was accustomed to from a lifetime in western America. As they approached the airport, no other planes could be seen anywhere, even sitting idle on the tarmac. Then he saw the runway: Jim was no stranger to travel, and that was the shortest, most rundown runway he had ever seen. Karen caught the look that passed over his face and just smiled, while cupping his chin in her hand, and said, "Now listen here, Jim Callister. We are here for a reason. We aren't going anywhere until we've done whatever it is that we came to do. The kids need to see that you're okay with all of this, so buck up and trust your wife, eh?"

Jim turned his eyes away from the round window of the airplane and to his wife's clairvoyant face. She beamed with self-assurance. She knew from deep inside that she was close to something very special, something that only her family could help her accomplish, something that seemed destined by forces working together on their respective continents. She was so self-assured and yet so focused on everything outside of herself. And she was just so incredibly beautiful to him right now! He looked at her in awe, as if he were seeing her for the first time and yet knowing that he had seen her like this for literal millennia.

He was just moving in to kiss her—he really had no choice to do anything else given the magic of the moment—when suddenly the plane bounced on the runway, Johanna let loose with a little shriek, Karen's head jerked forward and butted Jim right on the nose, and the magic fled—nearly as fast as Jim lost his ability to think clearly. As the pilot applied the brakes, the plane continued to bounce across the incredibly uneven though paved runway. The Callister children joined a number of other guests who gasped at every unexpected bounce, while Jim and Karen just laughed at bumping heads and at the thrill of being so close to their objective. When the plane came to a halt, everyone on board broke out in a spontaneous cheer of congratulations to the captain for a job well done.

Jim, Karen, and Rick helped the girls and then themselves to retrieve their smaller bags from the overhead luggage bins. When everyone was ready and it was their turn to walk down the aisle to disembark, as if on cue everyone drew a deep breath and looked at Karen, the mastermind and driving force. "Well," she said, "we'd best be on our way, don't you think?" Then showing everyone her cheeriest smile, Karen did a neat turn on one foot and took off for the front of the plane, followed by Lucy, Rick, Johanna, Alice, and Jim.

Immediately as the little troupe made its way into the terminal, they noticed that it was smaller than any other that they had been in on the journey thus far. Rick glanced up at a list of flights on the wall—theirs was the only arrival showing for the entire day! In fact, it would be leaving again just as soon as it could refuel and load a new set of passengers and their bags. "Well, at least we won't be confused with all the other six thousand tourists in the airport today," he observed. "So where next?"

Jim looked about the terminal to get his bearings and look for signs. Fortunately, the signage was in both Cambodian and English, although one might wonder if it really was English. As with many Asian translations into English, some of these were quite curious. Over a food vendor, for example, was the sign: "Lively, decaying morsels!" Another had a picture of a bus, with the words: "Tootle because walking." Despite the obvious confusion and his need to find clear directions, Jim had to smile.

Most of the passengers were headed towards what seemed to be Customs, which seemed to be situated vaguely on the left side of the exit way. A few well-traveled businessmen walked briskly to the right of the crowd, bypassing the small crowds that began to form as numerous officials questioned the passengers, asking for papers and gesturing towards their baggage. Mike, their in-country contact for this trip and who was probably waiting in the lobby for them right now, had been quite clear in his letter:

"They will try to usher you to the left, but stay right!"

Well, Jim thought, *they certainly seem to be moving faster on the right. I guess Mike knows his stuff.* "Okay, gang, let's be on our way. Just keep to the right, even if they tell you to go left. Maybe they have a speed-check Customs gate on the right up here or something." And off they went, this time with Jim in the lead and Karen bringing up the rear. As they approached a rather wide gate through which all the passengers were walking, Jim headed directly to the right side. Immediately a uniformed employee stepped up and gestured to the left. Jim did not hesitate but stayed right on course.

"Dad! I'm pretty sure that he wants you to walk on the other side of this hall," Johanna whispered.

"I got that impression too, honey, but Mike told me that we had to stay on the right. He didn't tell me why, only that it was important to do so. So I'm going to stay on this side until I can go no further."

"We've got your back, Dad," Rick offered. "We'll come visit you in your bamboo prison every Tuesday afternoon—at least until we go back to the States. Then maybe they'll let you read a postcard once in a while."

"Real funny! Just follow me, okay?"

The gesturing man was now joined by two more, who began speaking rather loudly to Jim in a language that obviously none of the family understood. Jim hesitated for just a second, then continued forward holding firmly to Alice's hand as she followed just behind him, as if he believed that they might make him change direction but they would never bother a little girl. Ahead several more uniformed men noticed the Americans and called to their comrades, who called back a rather heated reply and gestured in Jim's direction. Apparently they had had enough, and the Great Callister Rebellion at Phnom Penh was quickly put to an end. Three uniforms stepped forward resolutely directly in the family's path and pointed to the left. There would be no passing them without making Rick's banter about bamboo prisons into a full-blown prophecy.

Defeated, Jim turned to his little band of followers, shrugged his shoulders, and followed the collective fingers pointed to the left. *That's where most of the people are anyway,* Jim thought to himself. *I'll have to ask Mike about this when we see him.*

Clarification was not long in coming, at least to some extent. An airport employee escorted them to the Customs window, never leaving their side for an instant. Behind them in the hallway, various passengers were still being queried by officials. Some of the passengers seemed quite upset, and although the Callisters did not understand the language, the universal language of raised voices and body posture communicated their displeasure clearly enough.

"Passports?" the thickly accented voice requested. Karen opened her handbag and produced six American passports. Painstakingly, the officials behind the counter examined the documents, comparing photos with actual faces, pointing at various stamps in Jim and Karen's passports and then chattering on for minutes, leaving the two parents wondering whether they had traveled in some enemy country and were therefore in danger of being refused entrance. After close to fifteen minutes, the uniformed officials turned back to the family and pointed to the straining baggage, gesturing that they should lift the bags onto a table and open them for closer inspection.

Inwardly Jim groaned. He knew what an effort it had been to force those bags closed after filling them beyond capacity with quilts, candy, sanitation kits, and other gifts, as well as their own clothes for a trip halfway around the world to a completely foreign environment. But what could he do? Resigned, he simply watched as reinforcements were brought in to open each bag they owned, regardless of size, to paw through the contents, disheveling Jim's ordered arrangements, then turning to each other for repeated lengthy discussions. With each passing minute, combined with the unusual heat and humidity of the Cambodian air, the Callisters became more restless and more concerned. Karen in particular noted the interest that several men took in their daughters' clothing and tried hard to hide her concern at the lengthy looks that some of the younger men sent the girls' direction.

Most of the other passengers had passed through Customs by now, yet the Callisters were still being kept. At last, one of the uniformed men, probably chosen because of his English skills, approached Jim, passports and a stamp in hand. "James

Callister—one hundred dollars please!" he stated firmly.

"I'm sorry—did you say one hundred dollars? For what?" Turning to Karen he reiterated, "One hundred dollars so we can enter the country? I didn't know anything about this."

"James Callister—one hundred dollars, stamp passport, enter Cambodia." Jim was not so innocent as to not know that the clear cut rules of American travel were not universal. He had actually brought a fair amount of cash, most of it secreted away in several hidden pockets throughout the luggage and personal items of his family. If one bag were stolen or lost, they would still have the money in the other ones. And he expected as an American to be somewhat taken advantage of. But this?

Karen was silent for a minute, then whispered, "Pay the money, Jim. It's not worth causing a big scene and jeopardizing anything. What's a hundred dollars anyway—you can barely get a hamburger and fries for much less than that these days!"

Jim swallowed and pulled out his wallet. He turned slightly to hide the full contents of his wallet from the officials in front of him, selected a more worn hundred dollar bill, and handed it to the English-speaking official. He, in turn, put the money in his pocket, stamped Jim's passport, and handed it over. Then he turned to Karen. "Karen Callister—one hundred dollars please!"

Jim nearly swallowed his teeth! "I just gave you a hundred dollars to get us into the country. This is ridiculous!"

The man just looked at Karen and smiled. "Jim Callister now in Cambodia. Must leave airport. You come to? One hundred dollars, stamp passport, enter Cambodia." Then, to really drive the point home, he pointed out through the airport windows at their plane taxiing down that excuse of a runway, preparing for takeoff. "Last plane leaving. Better stamp passport."

They were had! Jim understood now that he had passed through Customs and was going to be required to move on. If they wanted to stay together, there was nothing he could do but pay their ransom. There was nothing else to do.

A few minutes later, with his wallet six hundred dollars lighter, Jim was then pointed to the baggage. Not one Customs officer, if that's what they really were, had attempted to straighten the contents after their rough searching. It took another 15 minutes of combined family effort to get everything put back together and properly buttoned up. Johanna noted wistfully that they were the last ones to leave Customs.

"At least we can finally meet Mike and be on our way!" Karen said brightly as they walked through the exit doors. "He said he'd be waiting right here in the parking lot outside the terminal."

Lucy was the one to state the obvious: "Mom, the parking lot is pretty much empty, except for those three very non-Mike-looking Cambodian guys under that tree over there who keep staring at us. And they're starting to creep me out!"

Jim and Karen looked to each other for comfort—and both came up dry. "I guess we're not out of the woods yet, Callisters," Jim ventured. Thinking of RP's warning, he continued, "We need to just keep our wits about us. We're in a country where no one understands us, our guide is a no-show and may have mislead us into having to pay a lot of money because we upset the Customs officials, and the only plane in the airport has already left. For all we know, 'Mike' may not even be within ten thousand miles of Cambodia."

Karen agreed. "Your dad's right. We need to be smart and not jump to any conclusions here. I think it's time for a Callister family moment. Let's put our bags together so we can sit on them in a little circle." Even Alice understood what "Callister family moment" meant. Jim and Karen had always been religious, but even more than that, they were deeply spiritual, and they had taught their children to rely on spiritual powers whenever they were in need. When intense challenges faced one or more of the family, they would gather together in a small circle, hold hands, and silently and simultaneously pray for a proper resolution. It had helped on previous occasions, and it seemed exactly the right thing to do now.

So in a nearly empty parking lot in Phenom Penh, Cambodia, six Americans joined hands while seated on their nearly bursting luggage and bowed their heads. As they did so, the roar of an incoming car engine threatened to disturb their peace.

"Hello there, Callister family! Welcome to Cambodia!" Six heads snapped up and looked around. Attached to the voice was a handsome, tanned, and somewhat muscular young man in his thirties, leaning out of the window of an approaching passenger van. "I'm glad you haven't given up on me and gone off on your own! I'm Mike. Mike Johnson."

In short order, introductions were made, hugs were exchanged, and baggage was loaded into the luggage rack atop Mike's van. As the girls climbed into the waiting vehicle, Jim's eyes ran involuntarily back to the three men Lucy had mentioned earlier. Though they appeared to be having a discussion, Jim was alarmed at how focused their eyes were on Karen and their girls. As Jim seated himself next to Mike in the front of the van, though he tried to chat lightly with Mike, he noted with alarm that the men also got into a nondescript cargo van and pulled out of the lot just twenty seconds behind, headed in the same direction.

RP's warning rang in his head.

Chapter 9

"So, Mike, what was the bit all about when you told us to stay to the right for Customs? I tried to do what you said, but the Customs officials insisted that we join everyone else on the left. And I ended up spending a hundred dollars per person just to get our passports stamped? Is that normal? I've never had to do that when we've gone to South America or Europe, but I have no experience in this part of the world."

"Sorry, I should have explained that better. Actually, I wish I could meet people when they just get off the plane and help them through that whole Customs process, but as Americans, if you got through with only a hundred dollars per person, you did better than some. Probably better than most. The thing is that everyone has to go through Customs, right? And the locals know that Americans and Europeans who travel here probably have money—at least more than they are used to from local travelers. They also know that you probably don't speak the language. So if they can slow you down any way they can so you start to worry and get tired and anxious to move on, you'll be more willing just to lay out whatever cash they demand just to get on your way.

"They've developed quite a system, but the locals know that if you stay to the right, you can bypass most of the delaying tactics and move right up to the Customs booth to do the necessary business and then be on. Unfortunately, you and your family really don't look very much like traveling Cambodian businessmen and dignitaries, so despite your best efforts, they still brought you into their system in the end. Still, your knowing enough to try to get past the earliest stalling tactics probably made them think that you have local connections. That's why you got off with a smaller bribe than some have to pay. Last month, I heard of one poor couple from Germany who dressed a bit too well for traveling here; they coughed up $225 each before they got their Rolex watches and Italian leather shoes through the gauntlet. Nobody gets through without paying something, myself included, but knowing the system can save you a week's lunch money anyway."

Mike then turned slightly in his seat and proceeded to give the entire family an unofficial tour guide's description of his route from the airport to our first official visit: a meeting with a family support organization. Once a month, this group from around the city came together to share successes and look for ideas to serve better in their individual communities situated about the city. The purpose of the organization was to provide support to people interested in strengthening their families. The fascinating thing about their structure is that it was actually made up of whole families, not just interested adults as they would have found in America.

As the Callisters pulled up outside the meeting, which was being held in a community center, Mike warned them that they were arriving late. As inconspicuously as possible, they slipped in through the door and made their way to some open seats. Of course, as they did so, every head in the room turned to see who was coming in so late (apparently punctuality is valued in Cambodian culture). An American family stood out as clearly as mud splashed on a freshly painted white fence.

Even among Americans, the Callisters stood out. They walked with the ease of natural athletes who knew what it was like to work hard and accomplish much. Jim led the family with his fair skin and red hair, not a common sight in this country of darker complexions and black hair. The rest of the family followed, all attractive by Western standards, confident yet humble, a bit travel weary but very attuned to their surroundings. A subtle entrance was out of the question.

Nonetheless, the meeting went on. The Callisters understood nothing of course. People stood and seemed to give reports. Sometimes a brief discussion ensued. Everyone was polite and gracious to one another. And the Callisters sat and listened—and sweat profusely. The temperature was by now hovering between 85 and 90. Karen whispered down the line that air conditioning was probably a luxury to be found nowhere in the country. And Lucy was convinced that the humidity was at least 160 %, if that were possible. Poor Alice just sat next to her mother and melted, stuck to her like a pair of popsicles on a too-warm day. Several people seated close by passed hand fans over to the suffering family, miming how to open and use them to create a small cooling breeze. Though hardly the air conditioning they were used to, the fans were nonetheless very helpful, and the Callisters smiled and nodded in profuse gratitude for the thoughtfulness. Even little Alice waved her hand weakly to show her thanks for saving her life from certain death as a pool of liquid girl in a foreign country.

Forty minutes after they entered the room, the meeting came to a close, and the Callisters became the most popular item on the menu. Thankfully, Mike stepped up and acted as family representative and occasional interpreter, carefully balancing interaction with protection. For their part, the family found the Cambodians in the room to be gracious, sincere, and appreciative. Mike told the locals that the Callisters had come to conduct humanitarian service, and the response was clearly moving.

And then it was over, and Mike led them back outside to the van and lunch.

Alice was the first to speak. "Lucy, look at all these guys leaving the building. How do they fit like that?" The "that" Alice referred to was a scene that would become very common to the visitors in the days to come. Father, mother, and children would all climb onto a single scooter in the most amazing balancing act and take off down the street. It was as if the entire country were made up of circus performers. Every spot on each scooter that could support a person was used—and many spots that should not have been but were!

"Check that one out to the right!" added Rick. "Dude, I just watched eight people climb on to it, although I still don't know how they did it or how they're staying on."

"I can't imagine how many people must get hurt every day from falling off their perch on one of these little scooters in the middle of traffic," added Karen.

Mike picked up right on cue, "Actually, I think you'd be surprised how rarely that happens. It's like a lot of things in life—it just depends on what you're used to. For people here in Phenom Penh, they grow up riding around with ridiculous numbers of people on these little scooters that they use, but they start doing it before they can walk. It's second nature, although you'd very quickly get arrested if you tried that on any major street in a U.S. city! Now pile in—we've got a real treat in store for lunch, so we don't want to be too late and miss out!"

Five minutes later, Mike pulled into a small parking lot next to an outside restaurant. "The owner is originally from Seattle," he explained. "He's a great guy and has been very supportive of our efforts here in the city. He will often donate food and other goods to those who need it. Let's go meet him."

"So this must the Callister family you were telling me about," said a voice from the shadow at the front of the restaurant. Then the voice emerged, revealing a rather diminutive, slim man with a smile as wide as his torso with hands extended to welcome his visitors. "Any friend of Mike's is someone worth knowing! Please, come, I have reserved two tables where you can watch our unique street scenery and yet not be in danger of being run over by an errant street merchant. Come, come."

As soon as they were seated, a waiter came by with a few well-worn menus. Not that they were any help—they were entirely in Cambodian. Not a word in English nor a picture to help them. "Let me help you with the menu," Mike offered. "Although the food here is really great, your taste buds are probably not quite ready for some of the items listed. For example, I would avoid the pizza. It's got an herb that they use for seasoning that gives a good flavor, but from what I know of your family, you'll want to stay away from it."

"Okay, Mike," ventured Jim. "You've got our attention. What is this secret herb?"

"You would know it as MJ, Mary Jane, weed, or just plain old marijuana."

Jim smiled wryly as Johanna's jaw dropped in disbelief. "Say what?"

"Yeah, laws in Cambodia are a little different than in the U.S., but getting caught with the drugs that are against the law bring very, very stiff penalties—even up to life imprisonment. And you do not want to experience prison life in this country. The worst prison in America is like a cheap hotel compared to what you get here. Anyway, I'd just suggest you don't get the pizza—for several reasons. But the pork noodles are very good. Hard to go wrong with them."

Not surprisingly, seven orders of pork noodles were ordered when their waiter came back around. The herb pizza had squelched their sense of culinary adventure for the time being. As they waited, Mike began to fill them in on their schedule for the next several days. "In addition to doing a great deal of good for some very needy people, I think you're going to have some fun here. We'll start off with a hospital for children with AIDS, where you'll get to paint some rooms and provide them with some of the supplies that you brought with you. We will also be teaching some farming techniques and animal care in a nearby village, and providing some much needed help at several orphanages. I promise, you'll fall so in love with these little kids that you won't find the language to be a barrier at all. Let's see, after that we'll be with the Red Cross to hand out wheel chairs and work in a relocation camp. And, lest you think that all you're going to do here is eat weird food and do a lot of sweaty work, I've also got some light sightseeing built into the schedule. But this is sightseeing unlike you've ever seen before—a little can go a very long way. It will change your life, just wait and see."

Little did Mike know how prophetic his words would be for this young American family.

Just as they were finishing their lunch, which met with various reviews by the kids in particular, they were astonished to see an elephant lumbering down the street. A vendor was walking it to the river across the street for a drink of water and a few refreshing squirts from its long trunk. "Mom, let's go see if we can pet it!" Alice nearly squealed. She had always had a fascination with elephants, so to see one this close was a dream come true.

"Mike, is that kind of thing allowed here? We don't know the customs . . . would that be taboo to venture over to see the elephant?"

"Of course not! Let's go check it out, Alice. I think that's a great idea. The rest of you want to come with us?"

Unanimous smiles jumped to six tired faces, and they all stood to follow Mike. "Hold on a minute," Jim said. "Let me just pay for lunch, and we can all go elephant admiring together."

As if by magic, the owner of the little restaurant appeared at their tables. "Oh, no you don't! Can't have that at all. We get so few American visitors that I would be delighted if you would accept my gift of a few poor noodles on this first day of your visit. Just make sure that you tell all your friends to come see me when you get back to the States, yes?"

"You've got yourself a deal! Free advertising is the least we can do for such gracious hospitality. Thank you so very much!" A chorus of thanks rang out from the rest of the family, and then they were off to the river. Mike approached the street vendor who was caring for the animal and chatted for a minute, obviously explaining that this American family had traveled halfway across the world to see his elephant. Could they please pet it?

The older Cambodian gentleman broke into a warm smile and gestured to the family. Alice went first, not surprisingly, and for the next fifteen full minutes they stroked the huge animal as if it were their favorite puppy.

But while the rest of the family was watching the antics of the elephant, Jim's eyes were covertly focused on three Cambodian men standing next to a very used cargo van about sixty yards up the road.

Chapter 10

"And this, my new friends, is your home while you're here in our lovely country," as Mike gestured towards a wooden frame house that, while very modest and sorely in need of paint, was not made of corrugated tin or plywood. *Very nice!* thought Jim. *We're going to be alright!*

As the troop approached the structure, most of their bags in hand, a young man stepped from the front doorframe and began to approach them, moving ever so slightly in Mike's direction. "Fantastic! You're here!" Mike called. "This day just keeps getting better and better! Callister family, please meet one of my best friends, Tree. And Tree, meet a tremendous family from the United States, the Callisters—Jim, Karen, Rick, Lucy, Johanna, and Alice. Tree will be your driver, interpreter, guide, and culinary adviser for the next two weeks."

"So pleased to meet you, Callister family," the young Cambodian said in understandable but accented English. In his early 20s, he stood about five feet five inches tall, weighed maybe 120 pounds, sported a bowl haircut for his straight black hair, with light khaki pants and a loose fitting button-up shirt left untucked from his beltline. On his feet he wore well-worn sandals ("Jesus shoes," the kids called them). "I hope you will have a most wonderful time in our country. We are pleased that you chose us to visit with your desire to do good.

"I will leave you for now to get acquainted with your sleeping quarters—I believe you will need sleep after a full day of travel and whatever else Mike has made you do today. But I will return at half past seven tomorrow morning to begin your day with you. We have very full day, so please sleep well, and I will see you all tomorrow!"

Nodding politely to all, Tree walked over to a nearby scooter and smiled back at the Americans while he climbed on. Easily starting the engine with the kick start, he sped away towards the nearby busy intersection to join the hundreds of similar travelers already on the main street.

Alice tugged on her mother's hand, wide eyed and looking a bit concerned. "Mom! Are we going to all have to fit on that scooter tomorrow like other families that we saw today?"

The rest of the kids couldn't help themselves. It had been a long day, and Alice's question put them over the top. They fell in a giggling heap on the ground at the notion of the Callisters all piled onto Tree's diminutive scooter. Visions of the photos they could send home to their friends flashed through their collective heads the way only siblings can do. "How about it, Mike? Alice is wondering whether we will be traveling about the country with our bags of goodies and all hanging on Tree's scooter."

"Alice, I'm sorry to disappoint you, but he's actually going to drive you in my van. Although if you really want, we can change our travel plans and attempt the scooter," Mike winked at Karen as he teased Alice.

"No, I don't think that would be good at all, Mr. Mike. The van will do nicely, thank you."

"Well, if you're sure. And with that vital decision made, I will take my cue also to bid you good evening. I think you'll find the accommodations simple but comfortable. Please make sure that you securely lock all the doors and windows before you go to sleep. The windows can be left slightly ajar because of the bars on the windows, but remember you are Americans in a foreign country, and that means some people will consider you as an easy target for theft. Just be smart, and you'll have nothing to worry about.

∞ ∞ ∞

Despite being bone tired the night before, the Callisters were awake at seven o'clock and were dressed and waiting when Tree pulled up in front of their house precisely as he had promised. As they climbed into the car, he handed Karen a bag of fruit to pass around for breakfast. The fruit was unfamiliar but mostly satisfying, and frankly they were all very grateful for something to eat. Little did they know that they would recognize very little that they would eat for the next two weeks.

Within minutes Tree pulled up outside a small local hospital.

The one-story structure was old and worn, the stucco-covered walls painted at one time the usual drab white that seems to be the universal color of all older hospitals—except for the salmon pink ones that tended to break all the normal rules. "Here we are," Tree announced. "This morning we are meeting with Dr. Jorani, the resident doctor in charge of this facility. You must know that this is not a typical hospital. This is a hospital where children who have AIDS are taken care of while they wait to die. There are several such hospitals in the city, but this is one where we have done some work recently. I think you will find the morning most interesting!"

Already a line had formed that extended from the battered wooden front doors, down the street, and around the block—twice! Jim couldn't believe there was such a line so early in the morning. "Tree, what are all these people doing here? I see more than just children in line. Didn't you say this was a hospital for children?"

"Well, yes, but people know that this is a hospital with a reputation for mercy. These people all need help of some sort; many have probably been waiting in this line for days, hoping that they will get inside before it's too late. The hospital does the best it can, and it takes care of many more than they are supposed to, but they cannot take care of everyone. So people come and wait. And they try to hope when they have little reason to hope, because that is all they can do."

Tree escorted them up the sidewalk, past the lines of waiting and dying people, and through the front doors of the hospital. They had barely walked into the entry way when a middle-aged Cambodian woman wearing well-worn hospital scrubs approached them. "Greetings! I am Dr. Jorani. You must be the Callisters. I am so pleased that you were able to come to our little hospital today. As you can see, we do not have much, but we do what we can."

"You have excellent English, Dr. Jorani. I'm very impressed!" began Jim.

"I thank you, Mr. Callister. I studied medicine at UCLA when I was younger. I have not yet forgotten all that I learned there."

"Please, call me Jim. And this is Karen, and our children,

Rick, Lucy, Johanna, and Alice."

Karen piped up, "We would like very much to help you in some way, Dr. Jorani. We have brought some things for the children you work with, but is there anything else we can do while we are here today?"

Behind the doctor in the nearest room were perhaps thirty children. Many of them had a purple swath of paint across their foreheads. Karen continued, "Tell us about your children here. Why do so many of them have that purple paint on their heads? Does that mean something bad?"

"No, actually its meaning is quite positive. Our nurses mark the children in this way when they have received their medication. Although they are dying, the medicine will help them go more peacefully when their time comes. That's all we can do for them."

If the outside of the hospital was run down, the inside was nearly dismal. The yellow and red tiles that lined the floors and hallways were stained and cracked. The rooms were less than sterile by anyone's standards, let alone those of the medical profession. Roaches scurried about the corners, and the ever-present flies seemed to be having a convention at the expense of the children. The beds were rickety cribs, with boards for mattresses. No bedding could be seen for any of them—no sheets, no blankets, not even a pillow. Space was so limited that some of the cribs held two weakened children instead of one.

"Come, let me show you where our children spend their final hours. I hope it will not be too much for your little Alice?" Dr. Jorani said, half in question.

Dr. Jorani walked them down the two hallways of the hospital, with approximately eight rooms of varying sizes. Not only were the rooms occupied by small children and adults alike—emaciated and weakened, in obvious pain and unattended in their final hours, but the walls were graying and smelled of death. All in all, they were rooms that were more conducive to depression than passing into the next life, freed at last from pain and sorrow.

"Well, Callister family, do you think there is anything you could do to make these rooms environment that would be more positive for our suffering children and their parents?"

Karen looked at her children, "What do you think, kids? Can we help them out?"

"Let's do it!" "I've got some ideas already, Mom." "Is there somewhere that we can buy some paint and brushes?" Excited voices shot out immediately, relieved to have the chance to do something constructive instead of just observe the pain and suffering.

Tree responded, "I thought you might ask that. I know just the place to take you, and we won't even need the van."

A five-minute walk brought the Callisters and their guide to an open shopping center. Even Dr. Jorani broke away from her work long enough to come with them, leaving the hospital in the hands of her nurses. Shopping was a blast! Tree translated for them and helped to negotiate prices as they selected both painting and medical supplies.

"Hey, Mom! Look what we have over there!" Johanna was so excited she could hardly stand it. "We've got to check out those shops before we leave. Please!" With a little arm twisting, the girls convinced Rick and Jim to venture into their newfound shopping mecca. Hundreds of people swarmed around them as they meandered through the shops. The morning sun began to beat down on them, and the heat and humidity was merciless on the Americans, but the adventure and newness of the market made them set aside any physical discomfort.

Right in the center of the market was a meat vendor. Nearly every kind of meat imaginable lay on the tables, and some that were not so imaginable: eyeballs, snakes, frogs, bugs, and anything else that walked, crawled, swam, or flew. To their surprise, not a single item was covered or cooled in any way. In fact, the only thing covering the vendor's wares were the constant swarms of flies.

Everywhere there were flies! Although the girls were absolutely disgusted by them, the local shoppers didn't seem to mind at all as they flocked around the meat vendor and bargained for his products. The Callister children in particular were utterly amazed at the vast quantities of meat that were purchased, but more than that was the shock at seeing what they considered to be really gross animal parts being bought for food. Also the complete lack of sanitation and the smell became deeply embedded in their senses, so much so in fact that from this point on they would eat no meat while in the country if they learned it came from a market such as this. Instead they would eat only bread or rice, fruits, and vegetables.

After the girls were finished with their "window shopping," they all headed back to the hospital, bags of supplies in their hands, laughing at the sites they had just seen and excitedly planning what they would do to the hospital when they got back to it.

Which wasn't long of course. Getting to the hospital took less than five minutes, and then the volunteers jumped right to their task. Lucy, who was an incredible freehand artist, began painting Disney characters on the walls of the children's room in bright and vibrant colors. As she did so, many children who belonged to the long line of sick adults outside heard of what she was doing, and a crowd of fascinated, giggling children began gathering outside the door of the children's room. While the rest of the family painted background colors and less imaginative bands of color on the walls, Lucy created new worlds for the children watching as she created in a way that they were obviously very unfamiliar with.

Alice caught the eye of a young child who seemed intent on following her every move. "She doesn't have long, Alice," one of the nurses whispered. "Perhaps another two or three days." Alice turned and walked directly to her, then extended her arms and gave her a warm and very lasting, sincere hug. Then, sensing that she had never had the chance to create with paint and color the way the Callisters were doing, she picked up the little girl and brought her into the room alongside the rest of the painters. Picking up a brush, she dipped it into a pint of vibrant green paint, brushed off the excess, and handed it to her new friend, gesturing that she should use it on the nearest wall in any way she wanted.

Unbelieving at first, she timidly touched the brush against the wall to see what it would do. The soft feathering of her touch left a light pattern of life on the wall, as if she were transferring some of what spirit remained in her damaged body into decorating the wall of the room where she would might soon pass away. Then her entire body broke out in a huge smile, if that were possible, and she dipped the brush again in the paint. Without stopping to gently wipe the excess, she dribbled her way across the floor and began making random strokes that—if you looked very hard and very creatively—somewhat resembled Lucy's characters. Magic had just happened in a hospital designed for death!

Karen looked at the crowd of young onlookers at the doorway and realized that she had an opportunity here that few mothers would ever experience. Gesturing warmly, she invited them in. They understood immediately what she had in mind, and came in without fear. For the next half hour, the Callisters helped a young band of angels create something so precious and lovely that the images would forever be in the minds of all who participated. Oh, they really were not very good at painting, and everyone got paint on themselves and each other, but the resultant artwork was exactly right for its purpose. Somehow the creative chaos unleashed in those few minutes captured the chaotic feelings of children who were too young to leave this world, especially doing so in unjust suffering. And yet there was also a sense of hope and life, of rebirth and new beginnings, and of a spirit that transcended mortality that spoke to them as only an image can, not bound by the restrictions of words.

For two days the Callisters cleaned, painted, and then cleaned again the rooms of that little hospital. Then it was time to move some new equipment into the rooms, and prepare everything for the grand unveiling. Dr. Jorani led her children, Pied Piper-like, through the front doors of this house of comfort and sorrow. Though the visitors from America could not understand a word of what the children said, their faces told the whole story—Jim, Karen, Rick, Lucy, Johanna, and Alice stood with tears streaming down their faces.

They knew they had made a difference, giving these and many more children to come some happiness during their final days and hours on earth.

Chapter 11

The morning after the Callisters finished their work at the hospital, Mike had scheduled them to visit a village in a remote part of Cambodia to teach the local people new techniques in farming and raising animals. Though the Callister family did not farm or own farm animals themselves, they had prepared well for this instruction through time at their local university's research division. They had also sought information about successful ventures in other parts of the world with similar growing conditions.

As usual, Tree picked them up from their temporary home bright and early in the van and joined the already heavy traffic on the main streets of Phnom Penh. They were soon outside the limits of the capital city where the roads were considerably less congested and found themselves winding past expansive fields of rice and endless palm trees. In the distance, they could see beautiful rolling hills. The haunting faces of the nearly dead whom they had met in yesterday's hospital began to fade in anticipation of today's adventure in agrarian innovation.

Rick seemed particularly thoughtful as they passed through the countryside. By nature a bit more introspective and quiet than his sisters, he was prone to drink a bit more deeply from the well of such an adventure as this than many others his age. Suddenly he tapped Tree on the shoulder, pointed due east, and asked quite seriously, "Tree, what is this structure that I see tucked back away from the road over there. I see people around it, but it doesn't seem be a house."

Their driver glanced quickly in the direction of Rick's gesture and a smile spread readily across his face. "I think that we have time for a brief stop this morning. Rick has pointed out what I consider to be one of our country's greatest treasures, and I would be wrong to not show it to you more closely." With that, he pulled into a small clearing at the side of the road that appeared to serve as a parking lot. Several scooters and an ancient panel wagon already occupied space there in an obviously unorganized yet thoughtful way, snugged over close to the trees to allow for additional guests to find place for a visit.

Tree led the family a short way up a well-worn path, wide enough to drive a small car on but obviously intended only for foot traffic. Ahead was a structure that resembled a half corn cob stood on end so that a rounded end rose toward the open sky. As they walked, Tree explained, "You will see two types of architecture with these temples: the Buddhist version is smoother as it narrows to the top, and the Hindu version looks more like steps that gradually get narrower and narrower. But the purpose of both is to honor the gods of each religion, and to help people show their respect to their gods."

As they approached the steps of the temple, they could see a family gathered together at the foot of the steps. Curiosity got the best of Lucy, and she sauntered off in their direction. When she got close enough to see what they were doing, she quickly gestured to her family to come join her.

"Tree, what are they doing? Is this a sort of ritual meal that they are eating?" The Callisters could now see that this family of eight individuals was sitting in a circle around a half-full rice bowl containing perhaps a single cup of rice. In turn, each person would place his chop sticks in the bowl and then place a purposefully small portion of rice in his mouth. The bowl would then pass on to the next, and the process would repeat. There was no clambering or grabbing to get an extra turn at the bowl, and the partakers were respectful and even reverent as they waited their turn there at the foot of the temple.

"No, Lucy, there is no such ceremony for us. This is simply a family who have come to thank the gods for the rice they have to share with each other. As you can see, it is not much when shared among eight, but it is important to be grateful for what they have—tomorrow they might have nothing, and then today's meal will seem bountiful."

Karen looked at Jim thoughtfully. "Listen, honey, would you go to the van and fetch that loaf of bread we bought at the market this morning. I think we've found someone who needs it more than we do today." All the Callister children nodded in agreement, even little Alice. In fact, she went with her dad to retrieve the loaf and then asked if she might be the one who gave the bread to this family at the temple steps. Jim consented, of course, and handed her the loaf, then stood back to watch how she managed.

Excitedly she walked towards their targets. "Excuse me," she said politely as she got closer. Several heads turned in her direction. "We have an extra loaf—" and then the unthinkable happened. Alice tripped over a rock that she had not seen in her quest to deliver her gift and headed face first towards the ground. But to everyone's delight, she simply tucked her head, deftly landed on the curve of her shoulder, and did a perfect forward roll, popping back up on her feet with the bread securely wrapped in her arms against her midsection. The Cambodian family could scarcely believe what they had seen and broke into spontaneous smiles and clapping. Little did they know that Lucy was already showing signs of an athletic gift for gymnastics and had been taking tumbling lessons for several years now. If the roll had looked practiced, it was because she had performed that basic maneuver over and over and over for months now. It was as natural as brushing her teeth.

Johanna, never one for shyness, jumped to Alice's rescue. "This bread is for you. Please take it." She took the loaf and handed it to the woman whom she surmised was the mother. She guessed correctly, and Mother recognized immediately what the girls intended with the bread and received it from Johanna graciously. But the younger members of the family were still focused on Alice.

Tree, who had been unaware of Alice's gymnastic talents, stepped forward and addressed the local family in their native tongue. "My friends wish to make this gift to you of a simple loaf of bread. They come from the United States and are seeking to learn more of our country and our ways. For the past two days they have been painting and helping improve a small hospital in Phnom Penh. They are good people. Thank you for accepting their gift." Tears formed in the mother's eyes as she replied, "Please thank them for their generosity. We came to the temple to give thanks and to pray for enough to eat today. Tell them they have answered our prayers."

Tree translated their message and then turned to the children, who were still watching Alice. Acting on an impulse, he said, "Would you like her to show you how she rolled like that without getting hurt?" Immediately their eyes widened, as did their smiles, as if that would be a treat far greater than any morsel of food. "Alice, these children would be delighted if you could show them how you were able to roll like that. Would you mind?"

Now it was Alice's turn to smile. For the next ten minutes she showed them some simple tumbling maneuvers that they could later practice and perfect on their own. Then Tree gently brought the visit to an end with a reminder that they still had a distance to travel, with more people waiting to benefit from a visit. Despite the obvious language barrier, much was communicated as the two families exchanged smiles and looks of deep gratitude. As Tree pulled back on to the road, Alice took one last look through the rear window, just in time to see the youngest boy execute a perfect forward roll!

The planned destination for the day was a remote village that could only be accessed by a very long, very dusty road. At one point, they encountered a farmer whose load had become stuck on a bridge. "Come on, gang, let's go help him get going again," Jim said. "For one, it's just the right thing to do, and for two, we can't cross the bridge ourselves until he gets off!" One wheel of his overloaded cart had become wedged in a gap on the old bridge, and the skin-and-bones ox that was attached to the front of it just couldn't break it free.

After the cart was loosened and the ox was once again trundling slowly down the road, everyone agreed that the scene reminded them greatly of the family they had seen on their first day getting onto a single scooter. Tree laughingly agreed, "We've been doing this for centuries, I suppose. Only the vehicle changes over time, not the method."

By late morning, the village was in sight, and apparently so were the Callisters. By the time the van arrived, the entire community had gathered in the large clearing in the center of the small structures that served as their homes. Tree handled the introductions humbly and openly, as he did all his communications. It was clear why Mike had chosen him as their guide: he was unassuming without being shy, witty and yet not a clown, street smart, and very likeable. His open confidence welcomed trust, which did much to pave the way for the Callisters' objectives.

After the formalities were concluded, Johanna headed up the effort to teach the village children some new games that they had likely never been exposed to before. Naturally outgoing, Johanna was in her element as she used gestures, smiles, and her siblings to generate a grand time. Before long, everyone was laughing and enjoying each other as if they were lifelong friends. Karen pulled out her camera and began taking pictures, which of course sparked immediate curiosity among the children. They were unfamiliar with such a device, so after Karen took a picture, she turned the camera around and showed the children the image in the viewing screen on the back. They could not believe what they were seeing as they recognized themselves in the small image! The astonishment on their faces was unforgettable as realization sunk in at just what they were seeing.

Meanwhile, Jim and Rick went with the men of the village to look at the rice fields. Though they had been growing rice here for generations, they were doing so using the same methods that their grandfathers and their grandfathers' grandfathers had used. With Tree's translation help, Jim explained some simple methods that were helping others to increase their yields significantly, methods that would require no additional cost and little labor to implement but would provide the village with better rice and more of it. They then did the same with their chicken and cattle, and ended with a simple booklet that visually demonstrated how to build wells for clean water. A reliable source for clean drinking water would alone have a significant impact on the health of the people and their animals, for now they were required to draw water from a small river using buckets, just as they had for years. In doing so, they were susceptible to whatever pollution had entered the water upstream.

The men of the village might not have been well educated, but they were certainly not unintelligent. As Jim and Rick explained these new ideas to them, they quickly understood the principles and excitedly discussed what it would take to implement their suggestions. Some could be done quickly and soon, whereas others, such as digging a well, would take additional planning in order to accomplish the task properly.

By now, the children had played themselves out and the men's heads were filled with new thoughts. It was early afternoon, and all the village gathered together for a simple communal meal. The Callisters joined in, cautiously avoiding anything that resembled meat, for the images of unprotected meat in the open market on their first day were still quite vivid to them. After eating, the visitors were shown a tour of several homes.

Simple structures, they were quite open to the elements in order to allow air to flow freely through them. Lucy was amazed to see that each one was no larger than the family room of their house in the States. The beds were nothing more than bamboo shoots placed side by side and doubled as tables during the day.

As they walked about, the women of the village showed their fascination with the American girls' blonde hair. They unabashedly stared at it, and many came up to them to feel it. Although at first a bit awkward, the girls quickly understood that the women meant no harm and allowed them to satisfy their curiosity as much as they wanted. The villagers were so open and honest in their emotions that it was impossible not to love them.

One troubling experience with the "tour," however, was that they encountered several sick persons lying in their huts. There was no real medical assistance to be had in the village, so the Callisters were unable to do anything outside of express their sympathy. Returning to the van, Karen brought out a large bag filled with hygiene kits. Though there was not much she could do for those who were already ill, perhaps the kits could help prevent some additional illness in the future.

As Karen handed out her kits to the adults, Johanna continued in her role as chief instigator with the children. She brought out a few bags of hard candy and, with the help of her siblings, began distributing it among her new friends. One boy about her age was hanging back shyly. It had become clear through the day that he was quite taken with the beautiful American and wasn't quite sure how to proceed. So Johanna pulled a rather large sucker from the bag and approached him with it. The villagers saw this gesture and began laughing, which didn't help his discomfort any. Embarrassed, he ran off, which only made the villagers laugh all the more. Johanna, for her part, thought it was a bit of a game, and took off in pursuit of the boy, which absolutely delighted their audience.

Once outside of the village proper, the young man slowed and turned to face his pursuer. In turn, she also slowed, holding out the sucker in an offer of friendship. Suddenly the light turned on in his eyes, and he recognized the gesture for what it was. Nodding his head slightly, he reached out to her and accepted the sucker, at which point she produced another just like it from her back pocket and began to unwrap the protective paper. From a distance, onlookers from both sides of the world cheered their congratulations as a friendship was born despite their inability to communicate with words. Johanna and her new friend worked through their suckers slowly and took their time coming back to join the rest of the village.

"Karen, my dear," commented Jim softly, "if more leaders around the world would learn to share a sucker as these two have, I think we'd be much better off. And I have a sneaking suspicion that what our daughter just did for this young man might just provide a boost of self-confidence and feeling of self-worth that will prove benefits for a long time to come."

Only one thing remained for the day to be called a success, and that was a safe journey home. As a fitting tribute to their fair-skinned visitors, the children in the village lined up to wave farewell as the van drove off. What the Callisters saw brought tears of laughter and of joy to each one, for grasped firmly in each small, waving hand was a new toothbrush, recently pulled from their hygiene kits.

They were making a difference.

Chapter 12

The sight of television cameras and reporters came as more than a slight surprise to the Callisters when they entered the room. Mike had arranged for them to meet with the Red Cross and assist in distributing wheel chairs to people needing them, but even Mike was not prepared for the media. Government officials, yes. But not this.

No one seemed quite certain how the media found out, but it really didn't matter. Mike supposed that some reporter had a connection in the government, and this seemed to smack nicely of a newsworthy human interest story: "American Family Works with Local Red Cross." In any case, when the Callisters arrived at the Red Cross building as planned, they were ushered into a room set up much as a board room. Also seated around the table were leaders from the Red Cross, officials from the Ministry of Health, and several people who looked like they could really use a wheel chair. The highest ranking official from the Ministry conducted the meeting while the cameras rolled.

Government officials the world over seem to have a similar problem: they talk too much and say too little. So it was with this little meeting—the fellow conducting the meeting wanted to ensure that he got plenty of camera time expressing the generosity of his ministry in working for the good of the less fortunate. At least that is what Tree explained to them as he translated quietly while the family gathered their chairs as close together as possible and leaned toward their new friend.

While the droning went on, Karen thought back on the morning's events. They had started at their usual early hour as Tree picked them up in the van and headed towards an orphanage run by an American, a Texan with a heart as big as his home state. Although he wouldn't share the entire story, he intimated that someone close to him had introduced him to a Cambodian orphan years ago, and he had found his life's passion. He was now dedicated to saving as many children as humanly possible, and he was doing an amazing job of it.

He had done much to prepare the children of his orphanage for the visit. Karen had been particularly impressed with the play that the children had presented. Absolutely amazing, actually. They acted out their lives before coming to the orphanage, living in the orphanage, and then their being adopted. At the conclusion of the play, the child actors came to her family and placed necklaces of flowers around their necks that they had made fresh that morning. Karen had never had a more precious necklace in all her life.

The young man who brought Rick his necklace brought more than just flowers. In some uncanny exchange of the unseen, this young lad bonded with Rick on a personal level. Rick quickly became something of a surrogate big brother to the boy, and for the remainder of the visit the two were inseparable. Karen had never been prouder of her children than she was of Rick at this point.

But the morning was not over. After they left this orphanage, with Rick's little friend following him right to the van door, they went next to another orphanage in the country. As the van arrived, the children ran out to greet them. Karen reflected on the meal that was prepared and waiting for them when they arrived. The Callisters sat down in a large room that served as the dining hall with all the children and staff from the orphanage, and a young girl was asked to say grace. Showing no fear whatsoever, she stood, bowed her head, and prayed. Tree interpreted the prayer—a prayer so pure and powerful that even Tree, a non-Christian, was moved to tears and struggled to find the words to match the spirit of the little girl's prayer. Her faith and gratitude provided a moment that Karen would never forget. The girls actually ate without questioning the meat and where it came from, and the remainder of the meal was simple but inviting. They all agreed that this was their favorite meal while in the country.

Following the meal, Lucy taught the children in the orphanage how to draw Disney characters. Just as Rick had connected so deeply with a young man at the previous orphanage, two young ladies here seemed to show a particular affinity both for artwork and for Lucy herself. For the remainder of the time, the gifted young artists stayed close to Johanna, watching her technique and copying it to the best of their ability.

Karen suddenly came back to the present as the government official turned to the Callisters and requested them to introduce themselves. Mike stood and spoke first in English, "They've asked for an introduction, folks. So as I say your name, stand and smile, okay?" With that, he switched to Cambodian and proceeded—on cue, each member of the family stood and smiled for the cameras.

Next the official invited one of the recipients of the wheel chairs to address the media. A woman stood with the help of a single crutch and began to tell her story. As usual, Tree provided the interpretation for the Callister family. "One day as I walked home from work in the evening, an automobile strayed from the road and struck me. My left leg was broken. When I went to the clinic to see what could be done, I was given two options: (1) the doctor could set the bone and cast the leg, but the cost for this procedure was 25 dollars, or (2) for only 7 dollars, the doctor would amputate my leg above the broken bone, and I would learn to live with only one leg. I am but a poor woman. Although I would have loved to keep my leg, I did not have the money for this procedure, so now I have but one leg. I look forward to receiving one of these beautiful new wheel chairs, for it will allow me to go many places that I could never go before." Turning in succession toward the minister, the Red Cross, and the Callister family, she thanked them for the gift, then awkwardly took her seat again. Karen was moved deeply, but the best for her was yet to come.

As a final act, Mike had arranged for a group of orphaned children to sing a special song called "A Child's Prayer":

Heavenly Father, are you really there?
And do you hear an answer every child's prayer?
Some say that heaven is far away,
But I feel it close around me as I pray.
Heavenly Father, I remember now.
Something that Jesus told disciples long ago:

"Suffer the children to come to me."
Father, in prayer I'm coming now to thee.

As the children finished, there was not a dry eye in the room. Even hardened journalists were weeping openly. Lucy leaned over to her mother and said, "Have you noticed that every child has a smile on his or her face, even when they are leading what we think is a hard life? They all seem to be happy, regardless of their circumstances."

"Often when people do not have what we consider to be necessary, they are nonetheless happy, Lucy." The Callisters finished the day understanding this principle as never before.

Chapter 13

"Mom, why are those men carrying guns? What's going to happen? I thought we were just going camping today!" Alice was obviously concerned by the sight of men in military uniform carrying semiautomatic AK 47s and extra ammunition in the belts around their waists.

"Well, dear, we're not really going camping. I'm afraid we must not have explained that very well. This place all around is called a camp. It's where people live who don't have a house or other place to call home. So they make these little shelters and hope for better in the future."

As Karen explained, she thought back to Mike's invitation to serve in this relocation camp for a day: "Although things are much better now than they were under Pol Pot's dictatorship in the 70s, the government still does things that I just don't approve of. This village is the result of one of them. If the government decides that they want a parcel of land that happens to be occupied, they just take the land and relocate the inhabitants to these camps. The conditions in the camp, however, attract mosquitos, and they carry disease. Children are especially vulnerable. We have obtained from charitable organizations in the United States a large number of good mosquito nets that need to be distributed. Could you take them for me to the needy villagers in the camp?"

Jolted back to the present by the sheer presence of so many people around them, Karen continued explaining: "Alice, the men have guns just in case of an emergency, and because they are in the army so they have to keep their guns with them. But they're nice men who are here to help us. Don't worry a bit about them at all."

The Callisters were led to a temporary shelter where they would pass out the mosquito nets. As they walked through the camp on the way to the distribution point, they handed out tickets for the nets, one ticket for each family. The conditions that these families were forced to live under were appalling. Lucy pointed to a small trench that ran down what resembled something more of a path than a street and pinched her nose as she said, "Yuck! Is that what I think it is?" Just then a small boy confirmed her suspicions by walking up to the trench and relieving himself in it, right in front of everyone! Karen quickly placed her hands over Alice's eyes, but she figured that the rest of the family would benefit from getting a first-hand view of living conditions in the camp.

Tree responded, "Yes, Miss Lucy, that is the village sewage system. When families are sent to live here, they are given a small plot of land approximately 10 feet wide and 15 feet deep. As you can see, they have come with only what they could carry on their backs from their homes, and here they build their new homes." Johanna looked in astonishment, for the "homes" consisted mostly of a sheet of plastic held up with whatever boards they could scrounge from the area. The water supply was a group of communal water buckets with Red Cross stamped across each bucket, and raw sewage ran through the "streets" in tiny streams. Flies were thick everywhere, and the open market that the residents had created in the middle of the camp made the meat market they had seen on their first day seem downright sanitary.

The distribution post consisted only of a few two-by-fours that held a sheet of plastic overhead—apparently for the purpose of providing shade to the volunteers. It was at best ineffective. The girls pulled the nets out of the boxes and handed them to Jim and Rick, who handed them to each family who presented a ticket. Despite the presence of the armed guards, every family who came through their post was orderly and polite—all 1500 of them! By the time they were finished, their arms were aching, but their hearts were full. Because of those nets, hundreds of children would stand a better chance of surviving their youth.

One final experience touched the family, but especially Karen as a mother. After they handed out the nets and were making their way back to the van, they looked inside one of the makeshift homes to see an amazing sight—a mother was about to give birth in the heat, the dust, the unsanitary conditions that were common to everyone in the camp. While Jim and Karen did what they could to make her as comfortable as they could, the children helped entertain her children so she would not have to worry about giving birth while tending her little ones.

The scene was absolutely unthinkable, and yet there they were, acting as midwives and nursery facility in the middle of a Cambodian refugee camp on the other side of the world from their comfortable home and medical facilities. They would never think of the miracle of birth again without the vivid images of that experience coming to mind.

Chapter 14

The next day started ominously. Jim glanced out of the front window of their temporary home while the rest of the family put the finishing touches on getting ready for Tree to come pick them up. No, no familiar van was in front of the house yet. But there, a hundred yards or so down the street and tucked against a battered street kiosk, was a sight that he had chosen to forget over the past several days. He almost missed them in the early hustle of the street—overloaded scooters carried too many people and too large burdens in hopes that they might earn enough money to survive another day.

But no, they were definitely there—standing casually around their scooters, three men dressed in drab colors chatted quietly with each other, frequently pausing just long enough to gesture towards the Callisters' house or make a comment; the others would then nod or disagree, and continue their quiet conversation. Though Jim was not a professional in this field, he could tell two things from what he saw: first, he recognized the men as the same three whom he had seen in the parking lot at the airport, and second, these men were accustomed to waiting and watching, and this was not the first time they had worked together.

But why? As soon as the question formed in Jim's mind, he knew he did not want to know the answer. RP had warned them rather pointedly about the flourishing sex trade in Cambodia, and now that he had been in the country for a week, he had a much better sense for the conditions that drove such a trade. He had seen the crowd that his daughters had attracted wherever they traveled and knew that they could bring a handsome price.

But what to do?

Jim knew he didn't want to frighten the girls, but he also needed some extra eyes on the situation. As if by design, Karen and Rick entered the room just then, talking about the plans for the day. "C'm here, you two. I have something I want to show you before the girls get here."

Rick gestured towards the window where his father stood. "What'cha got, Dad? A new record for people on a scooter?"

"Not quite. I just want to point something out for you two to be aware of. See that old kiosk down the street a bit? There are three guys standing next to it—"

Karen interrupted, "Hey, I think I recognize them. Weren't they the guys hanging around in the parking lot when we first got into Phnom Penh at the airport? It's hard to tell, but I remember feeling a bit uneasy about how much they kept staring in our direction."

Rick chimed in, "And I could swear I saw them at the market once. Do you think it could be them, Dad? Why would they be following us?"

"I'm not sure, Rick, but I would like you two to keep your eyes open for the rest of the trip just in case. Not everyone in this beautiful land is as good as the people we've been meeting with, and you have three sisters who are a real novelty with their fair skin and blonde hair. I don't want to alarm them, but just to be on the safe side I think that the three of us need to step up our alertness of what's going on around us. The most important part of dealing with a problem is preventing it in the first place.

"I don't know, guys, maybe it's just coincidence, but maybe not. Let's just be careful and I think we'll be just fine." Jim and Karen exchanged glances, and Karen was relieved to see in her husband's eyes a look of confidence that said he really believed what he had just told them—they would be alright if they just used their heads. And their eyes.

"Hey, what are you looking at?" Alice asked as she came into the room, followed closely by her older sisters.

"Just watching for Tree and the van, honey," Karen replied. "Last night when he let us off here, he threatened to make us all ride with him on his scooter today, so we're just watching to see if he really meant it."

"No way! That would be sooo cool," Alice squealed. "Do you think we could all fit? That would be fun!"

"Sorry to disappoint you, little sister," Rick replied. "Here he is now, and it looks like he's decided on the van." He pulled back the curtains a bit further to reveal the now familiar vehicle stopping directly in front of the house. Tree saw his new American friends all gathered at the window and waved, then got out of the van and started up the worn footpath to the house.

"Okay, gang, that's our cue. Everybody have their cameras and hats? It's going to be a warm one today, and I think we'll be outside for most of it." While Karen herded everyone out the door, Jim did a quick last survey to make sure that everything was in order—windows shut, appliances and curling irons all turned off, finally closing the door firmly and locking it securely behind him. As he turned towards the van, he ventured a quick look down the street. Whatever purpose the three strangers had had earlier, they were gone now.

For some reason, that didn't give Jim much comfort.

∞ ∞ ∞

Once in the van and safely on the streets, if one could ever really feel safe on the streets of Phnom Penh, Karen made an announcement: "Today, as you know, is going to be different from what we've done so far. We've been fortunate to be involved in some very important service projects that will not only help improve many people's lives, but in some cases also save many people's lives. These have changed our lives as a family. But today we're going to see some things that might also have a deep influence on our lives, but in a very, very different way.

"In the mid-1970s, about when your father and I were Johanna's age, a man known as Pol Pot led a revolt against the government. He was a follower of the Chinese Communist Party leader known as Chairman Mao and believed that Western influence was corrupting his country. As a result, he set out to get rid of any signs of that influence. He destroyed libraries and meeting places where people of intelligence could meet, learn, and talk about ideas contrary to Chairman Mao's communist teachings. He destroyed many of the beautiful temples in the country so that people could not show their gratitude to the gods or develop faith in a higher power for good.

"He also killed many, many people. In fact, most historians estimate that he killed at least two million people from his own country. Anyone who opposed him was killed. This morning we are going to one of the places where many people died. I just want to prepare you that it is a very important place for you to see. It might help you understand why we are so grateful to live in the United States and why it is so important to choose good government leaders who try to fix our country's problems the right way, not through death and destruction."

Tree was obviously moved by Karen's words. He cleared his throat and then spoke quietly: "In America, most people know of Adolph Hitler and the terrible things he did to the Jewish people. Pol Pot was like our Hitler. He killed so many innocent good men, women, and even children. I agree with your mother—although it is not a fun subject, it is important to learn about the genocides that have occurred on nearly every continent on this planet so you can learn to prevent such things from happening in the future. It is your duty."

The inside of the van was very quiet for the remainder of the drive. Even Alice sensed the gravity of what they were about to see and didn't break the silence with her chatter or singing. Because Choeung Ek, their destination, was but ten miles south of Phnom Penh and the traffic was light, as it usually was outside of the city, the drive was relatively short. After parking, Tree served as their tour guide.

"This area is known as one of the 'killing fields.' It is called that for good reason. Do you remember that I told you that Pol Pot was like Hitler? Although both men were very evil and responsible for millions of deaths, Pol Pot was especially cruel. He would starve and torture his prisoners and then bring them to places like this, where large open graves had been dug. Here his men would sometimes bind them and often would blindfold them. Then they would beat the defenseless people to death using clubs or axes. The lucky ones were merely shot and then tossed into the mass graves. The indentions that you see are where the bodies have decayed and the bones settled—if you were to walk across them, you would be walking on the bones of those poor, poor people.

"Do you see that large tree standing over there? The sign next to it calls it the 'killing tree.' If you look closely, you will see that outdoor speakers are placed among the lower branches." Tree's eyes misted, and he was unable to speak for several long seconds. "I am sorry. I cannot see this tree without thinking of my father's young cousins, who died at this tree. Pol Pot's cruel men would grab babies and young children by the ankles and swing them around, striking their heads against the tree and crushing their skulls. The screams of the children and other victims of torture were so loud that music was played over these speakers at high volume so that the soldiers could not hear their victims as clearly." Tree turned away. "You may walk closer to that place if you would like. I cannot. For me, it is still too painful."

Alice stepped alongside him and reached her little hand to take his. "I will stay with you, Tree. I like this Tree much better than that one!" He smiled at her joke and at the sincerity of her concern. Perhaps because she was a child, she was the only one who could smooth the waters of his troubled heart. Gladly he received her hand, and together they strolled off in another direction while Jim, Karen, and the older children walked soberly to take a closer look at the fields and the solitary tree with the ominous speakers lodged in it.

"Dad, why are all those sticks poking out of the ground over here?" asked Lucy. "There aren't many trees around here—did they cut them all down for some reason?"

"No, honey, I don't think they had to cut down the trees. Remember that these were fields, so the ground would have been clear already for growing crops. I'm afraid those sticks that you see are really bones, the bones of thousands of people like Tree was telling us about. If you look closely, some of them still have tattered clothes on, but not many."

"Dad, you're right. And look over there. There's a whole line of skulls still wearing blindfolds."

"Rick, don't try to scare your sisters," Karen warned.

"Ooh, he's right!" squealed Johanna. "Those are skulls, and they are wearing blindfolds. Gross!"

The Callisters wandered about for several more minutes, being careful not to walk on any of the mass graves while letting the reality of the place sink in. Placed at various viewing stations were signs in several languages, including English, that described the dark events of three decades ago. Gradually they made their way back over to where Tree and Alice were waiting—all except Karen. She stood alone by the 'killing tree' for another ten full minutes, motionless except for an occasional wiping of a tear from her cheek. At last she turned and joined her family. "Maybe it's because I'm a mother, but I thought I could hear the whispering of little children. Not the screaming of those who were being killed, but the quiet whispers of those who had already died, trying to comfort their mothers who were forced to watch before they themselves were killed. Though they suffered violent deaths, the children were fortunate that they did not have to endure the pain and starvation of their parents. Maybe they were the lucky ones, in an odd sort of way."

Jim pointed to a rounded structure with glass walls that stood off to the side. He thought it looked a lot like some of the small temples that they had seen along the roadside. "Tree, what is that?"

"Yes, I'm glad that you asked. That is a Buddhist *stupa.* A stupa usually contains old relics of significance. This particular stupa contains over five thousand skulls from those who died here. It stands as a monument to their deaths—both to honor their lives and to remind the living to never allow such atrocities again.

"Now, if you have not had enough, Mike suggested that I take you to a prison close by where Pol Pot kept some of the political prisoners before he had them slain. I think it would be another important thing for you to see."

Tree drove back to Phnom Penh and navigated the back streets briefly before stopping at what was obviously a prison—Tuol Sleng prison, code named S-21 during Pol Pot's reign of terror. A brief tour was available so Tree again served as interpreter.

When the Vietnamese Army invaded Cambodia in 1979 in a move to unseat the Khmer Rouge, they found Tuol Sleng prison empty. The prison staff had fled when they learned that their enemies were closing in, leaving behind photographs and other records of five years of terror. Approximately 30,000 inmates had passed through the prison during those five years. In his effort to subdue and retrain the nation, Pol Pot had determined that anyone who showed any signs of independence, intelligence, happiness, or passion should be jailed. While there, they were starved, tormented, beaten, and tortured in a variety of inhumane ways.

Here the Callisters did not linger. The morning was passing quickly, and they had felt enough gloom and misery for the day and were ready to move on with their experience. After the quick tour, Tree stopped the van at a convenience store, where they all bought sandwiches and drinks to go, and then they were off across the entire country of Cambodia for the ancient city of Siem Reap, home of the famous temple of Angkor Wat.

Chapter 15

The long afternoon drive across Cambodia was uneventful. As Tree drove the mostly empty roads, most of the Callisters dozed, drifting in and out like the sunlight that peaked through the forest that stood sentinel-like on either side of the road. But one Callister could find no rest—Jim was plagued with unsettling thoughts. He tried to close his eyes to relax like the rest of his family, and his head echoed with the warning voice of his friend RP: "Please, if you love your girls at all, as I know you do, do not take them to Cambodia! The risk is just not worth it!"

At last, about 45 minutes from their destination, Jim nodded off. Immediately his head swirled with dark thoughts and even darker shadows. He watched his dream evolve as if he were the lone spectator at a live theater. It was dusk, and his family was walking up the street together. Usually Karen and Rick were at the front of their group for safety reasons, with the three girls following, and Jim bringing up the rear. But this time, Tree was at the front of the family, talking sincerely while walking between Jim and Rick. Karen and her daughters chatted joyfully behind, strolling several paces behind.

As they crossed a side street that intersected with the main street they were on, suddenly the four girls stopped and turned almost as one to look down the side street. Then they took off in that direction at a very brisk pace. The boys continued on ahead, oblivious to the fact that they were suddenly alone. But what followed next made the hairs on the back of Jim's neck stand straight up, despite his state of sleep, for in his dream Jim watched helplessly as the three men he had seen that very morning outside their house came from seemingly nowhere and followed the girls down the darkened side street.

"Jim! Jim! Wake up! Are you alright? You shouted my name, but you're sound asleep. What's wrong, Jim?" Karen shook her husband's shoulder again, obviously concerned.

"Oh, it's you! Karen, I'm so sorry. I must have been having a bad dream." Jim knew full well what he had been dreaming about, for the images were still as vivid in his brain as if he had actually been watching the events happen. He leaned close and whispered in her ear, "I was probably dreaming that I was an international spy and you were in the midst of being my latest conquest!"

"Get a room, you two!" called out Lucy. "There are children present, you know!"

Everyone had a good laugh, including Tree, who cleared his throat when the laughter died down and announced, "I have been working for Mike five years now, and you are my favorite clients I have ever dealt with. Thank you for sharing your family with me. And now, we approach the city of Siem Reap, home of the famous Temple of Angkor Wat."

Within minutes they pulled up in front of the hotel where they would be spending the night. Tree helped them unload their luggage, and then said, "My friends, I will come by at nine o'clock tomorrow morning, after you have had a chance to eat your breakfast."

"But Tree," said Alice, with whom the translator had developed a special friendship since their time at the killing fields. "Won't you be staying with us?"

"No, my little one. It is difficult in my country, but I am not of sufficient status or class to stay at such a hotel. I will be in a small boarding house just down the street, don't you worry. I will leave the van here because the security is better at your hotel's parking lot, but I must not come in to this fine place."

At this, Jim spoke up. "I will not hear of it! Tree, either you stay with us, or we will find somewhere else to stay. We'll sleep in the van if we have to, but I will not allow you to be treated differently than our family. You have become like one of us."

"I thank you, Mr. Callister. But this is our way, and we have been doing it for centuries. I will be back in the morning," and with that he pointed out his night's lodging and took off walking.

"Dad, you can't let that happen. I'm sure the hotel will let him stay here if we just explain to them."

"That's exactly what I'm going to do. Kids, grab your luggage.

We're going to go do some international negotiations."

For 20 minutes Jim argued with the clerk at the front desk, who would not budge an inch. He demanded, he begged, he played the friendship card and the guilt trip—all to no avail. Finally, he turned and picked up his bags. "C'mon, Callisters. Let's go find somewhere else to stay the night."

Just then the hotel manager showed up from his inner office. "Mr. Callister, before you leave, I have one suggestion for you that might work. If you're willing to pay for another room, your driver may stay with your family."

Well, now we're at least getting down to what the real issue is for the manager. Sounds like one of Steven Covey's Win-Win scenarios—we get Tree with us and the hotel gets our money, Jim thought to himself, but he said aloud in reply, "Hmm, I suppose that we could find enough to pay for another room. Do you have one available that is close to the two that we already have?" When the manager nodded in the affirmative, Jim extended his hand, "We have a deal. Thank you for understanding our concerns and being willing to suggest a solution."

The Callisters quickly took their luggage up to their rooms, with Rick sharing the new room with Tree. As it worked out, Jim liked the arrangement, for he could be on one side of the girls with Karen, and Tree and Rick could be on the other. His earlier dream in the van had not completely left his mind. Then off they went in search of Tree's boarding house.

Fortunately, their destination was only four blocks south of their hotel. Though the sun was going down, they still had sufficient light to find the boarding house, where they quickly summoned Tree and allowed Alice to break the good news to him.

"Jim, Karen, and all of you. I do not know what you did to convince the hotel manager, but what you have done is nothing short of miraculous. I am so humbled that you would break centuries of discrimination for me."

"Tree, we told you that you were part of our family now. Where we come from, family sticks together. Now let's get going before we all start bawling like a bunch of babies." Jim threw his arm around Tree and directed him out the door and up the street. "Is it okay if you share a room with Rick here? He sometimes turns into a werewolf at midnight and eats whatever he can find in his room, but maybe we'll be lucky tonight. I don't see much of a moon coming up."

"I'll take my chances, Mr. Callister. I just might have some secrets of my own." Together they walked back towards the hotel, Jim and Rick bantering with Tree in the front of their little troupe, and the girls chattering away behind them.

As they were getting ready to cross the last intersection before reaching their hotel, Karen's head popped around quickly to look down the darkened alleyway. "Girls! Did you hear that? It sounded like a baby!" As her eyes adjusted to the lack of light, she saw something that made her blood curdle just a bit. A little bundle of blankets was sitting against the wall about 50 feet from the corner, and the sound coming from the bundle was clearly that of a baby. Two wild street dogs were closing in on the bundle, and Karen's motherly instincts were in hyper-gear. "Oh, dear! There's no time to lose—we've got to help that baby!" and off she jumped at a quick run down the alley, her daughters also concerned and close behind.

Jim thought he heard his wife's voice and turned his head to see what was up. Immediately his heart stopped beating, for what he saw was exactly what he had seen just an hour earlier in his dream on the van—as he turned he caught a glimpse of the three men whom they had seen their very first day at the airport, leaving the main street at a dead run. He knew that ahead of them were four of the most precious people in his world, and they were in a country known for turning just such girls into sex slaves. Suddenly his dream made so much sense. "No! This can't be happening! Rick, Tree, follow me! The girls are in trouble!"

Chapter 16

In one blinding flash, Jim's feelings of foreboding and warning made sense. And just as quickly, everything became confusing again.

Jim, Rick, and Tree burst around the corner, muscles throbbing with fear and adrenalin, ready to tear to pieces anything and anyone who stood between their loved ones and their freedom. But before them was a scene that didn't seem to make sense. You know how people say that when you face death, life slows down and everything moves in slow motion. That's exactly what Jim experienced as he turned the corner and prepared to knock some heads.

On the ground, laying against a building's outer wall was a bundle of blankets that was emitting crying sounds. Karen and the girls were standing next to it, but faced outward towards two men whom Jim hadn't seen in his dream. One of them held in one hand two leashes attached to two mangy dogs that were in process of being jerked back by that same man. The other brandished a knife, but was turning from the girls and towards the three men from Jim's dream.

With an angry thrust of the knife, he tried to cut the nearest of the three, who Jim could now see were clearly not part of the first group. Without hesitation, the would-be victim sidestepped the thrust, grabbed the knife hand, and in one quick movement broke the attacker's wrist and then spun and drove his elbow directly into the man's windpipe. Deprived of oxygen and in intense pain, the man dropped, almost beating his falling knife to the ground. The dog handler threw the leashes in the air and took off on a dead run. The two remaining men each grabbed a leash midair and deftly tied them to a nearby window railing, then turned towards the fleeing one. The man who had so efficiently dispatched of the knife handler barked out a couple of words that Jim didn't understand, but the two men looked at each other, shrugged their shoulders, and turned back to the women to see how they were managing. Then seeing Jim, Rick, and Tree approaching on a dead run, they stepped back in obvious deference—and to show that they meant the girls no harm themselves. And with that, life returned to normal speed.

"Jim! Thank heavens you are here. These men saved us—who are you? You look familiar, but how? Do you speak English? Oh, thank you so much!" Karen gushed more than spoke on the heels of their miraculous rescue.

The leader of the three strangers turned to Jim and Karen and spoke with a New England accent. "Yes, Karen, we do speak English. You were very fortunate that we were so close by. Those men had planned a very effective decoy to lure you away from the main street, but then they are practiced professionals. But first, I forget my manners. I must introduce ourselves to you.

"We are friends of a friend of yours. You know him as RP. We met him when he was here looking for his family several years ago, on his first trip. We too were looking for some missing family members. We have since traveled some very dark roads together in search of those we love, and RP has proven himself to be not only a good friend but also a very formidable ally in a tight spot. When he could not dissuade you from coming to our country, he called us and asked that we keep an eye on you—as a personal favor to him. We have been pleased to do so. I can see why RP thinks so highly of you, for you have done much good for the people in the villages and hospitals that you have visited."

And with that, suddenly Jim's world once again became clear and orderly. In true western American fashion, he went up to each of the three men, one at a time, and threw his arms around them in an unaffected display of gratitude and recognition. "You don't know how glad I am to hear this explanation. We have seen you several times since we came, but usually in the shadows and in what we thought were questionable circumstances." The three exchanged slightly embarrassed glances, as if to say, Oops! We didn't realize you had seen us! "When I saw you chase my precious girls down this dark street, I could only imagine the worst. I was ready to take all of you on myself to defend my girls—but after seeing how you treated this man with the knife,

I'm glad I didn't try!"

"Yes, I have had much training in such matters, Jim. I'm also glad that you didn't try." He winked at the girls as he continued, "I would hate to embarrass you in front of these lovely young ladies."

Karen stepped forward, shaken but grateful. "How can we repay you for saving us from . . . well, from those horrid men and their intentions, whatever they were? We are not wealthy, but please, name your price."

"Mrs. Callister, the only price that we would exact from you is the privilege of escorting your family back to your waiting hotel. It is enough that we were able to help friends of our friend, RP. We would do anything for him, as he would for us. Friendship knows no price. Besides, as I said before, we have seen what you have been doing for our country. This is the least we can do for the lives that you have saved and the much comfort that you have enabled. And did I overhear correctly? Has your husband worked some sort of magic to get your driver admission to the hotel as well? You are indeed a most curious and honorable family!"

"Whatever good we have done has been done with Tree's help. He should receive as much credit as you have given us, though it has been more of a pleasure to serve here than we ever imagined. And we would be very grateful if you would please accompany us back to the hotel. We would all feel much safer."

The little troupe walked slowly and for the most part silently back to the main street and then up to the hotel. In the lobby, each member of the Callister family hugged and thanked their three guardians. And before they retired to bed, Karen said thoughtfully to her husband, "You know, sometimes we pray to God for angels to help us, and sometimes he sends them in the form of regular people, just like us. I think that RP set us up with three of the best angels I've ever met!"

Chapter 17

Angkor Wat. Any attempt to describe the beauty and spiritual power that is inherent to that mighty temple will fail. On one level, it is a work of magnificent architectural achievement. On another, it is a cultural icon that has survived for over a millennium. On yet another, it is a spiritual center of world renown for Buddhist worship. The largest temple in the world, during its prime Angkor had been home to an estimated one million people. The fact that it still stands as the country's most visited site is physical evidence of Cambodia's regional power from the ninth to the thirteenth centuries. Today, the jungle dominates Angkor Wat, encroaching not only on its exterior grounds but also on to the structure itself. And yet, while all of these things are true and accurately describe the ancient temple, to see the temple walls in the early morning light invokes a reaction that far surpasses any and all of these facts as trivial.

Beginning with the events on the evening of their arrival, the Callisters were also quickly convinced that the temple of Angkor Wat is, if nothing else, a sacred place where angels move freely about to comfort, protect, and teach.

At breakfast, Rick pulled his mother and father aside for a minute. "Tree was amazing last night. I guess I didn't realize what an amazing thing you pulled off, Dad, when you convinced the hotel manager to let Tree stay with us. Did you know that last night was the first time that he ever slept in a bed, that he's never had air conditioning—in fact, he's never even had lights in his home. He was like a little kid at Christmas last night. He didn't want to go to sleep. He would bounce on his mattress, then turn the air conditioning on and off, and wouldn't let me turn the lights off all night long. The room finally got too cold for him so he turned the air off, but not those lights! And all he's talked about since we awoke was how comfortable it was to sleep on a mattress. Thanks so much for letting me share a room with him! I wouldn't have missed that experience for anything!"

Local vendors catered to the uniqueness of the site. When they found a man who gave elephant rides, the Callisters couldn't resist. What an incredible feeling it was to see the outer temple grounds while riding on an elephant! To realize that they were doing something that faithful worshipers had done for the past twelve centuries gave them a perspective on history that they could have received in no other way. They took turns taking pictures and posing with the gentle behemoths, knowing that their friends back home would never believe they had done such a thing without visual evidence.

When they had finished with their rides and picture taking, Jim and Karen were impressed that their children all reached into their pockets and gave the old elephant tender a tip from their own spending money. Maybe something was sinking in from this trip!

As the family walked up to the temple entrance, Alice suddenly grabbed Rick's hand and pulled him over to the side of the path. "Look, Rick! Isn't that a cool frog? It's different from what we have at home, I think. Look at him. He's checking us out, almost like he's making sure that we're safe to let into his temple."

Rick stepped over to where the frog sat and picked him gently up in his right hand. Then joining his other hand with his right to give the frog a larger and more sturdy platform to sit on, Rick turned to show his new friend to the rest of the family. He was too much of a gentleman to chase his sisters with it, but he certainly could show it to them.

Tree had stepped over to an information booth to get some brochures in English, and when he looked back he could see his American friends all gathered around Rick, but all the Cambodians who passed by and looked at what the young man had in his hands quickly scuttled to the far side of the path and hurried past. Curious, he walked quickly over to where the family was gathered. What he saw there drew all the color from his face and he knew he must take action quickly.

"Rick, please set that frog down—immediately! But don't toss it down or startle it in any way. Just gently set it down and move away." Rick had come to trust their guide and followed his instructions immediately. Once he had set it down, he looked quizzically at Tree for an explanation. It was not long in coming.

"Once again your god has provided you with a guardian angel! This frog is a special frog—highly poisonous. It had the power to kill all of you, even though Rick handled it quite freely. Clearly your purpose for coming to Cambodia has not been completed, or I would be rushing you to a hospital right now!"

Karen pulled a travel-sized container of hand sanitizer out of her purse, and Rick quite liberally applied it to his hands. Rubbing vigorously with all the energy that a near-death experience can provide, he quickly scrubbed any possible microcosmic organisms from his hands. Then he scrubbed again, and looked to Tree for confirmation that he would live to see another day.

"Believe me, you will all be just fine. If that frog had chosen to spit its venom on you, you would be quite aware of it by now. I truly think that you are watched over by guardian angels."

The family then entered the grand hallways of the temple and began the self-guided tour. Tree provided what information he could, and they were all fascinated by the statuary, paintings, and other cultural artifacts to be seen. Time flew by rather quickly—and then it happened.

4:32 p.m. That's when Jim first noticed that nine-year-old Alice was missing.

The tour had been one of the most incredible experiences they had ever had as a family, but right now it was the furthest thing from Jim's mind. Alice was not to be seen, and the scare they had had last evening was still painfully fresh.

"Karen!" he whispered nervously. "Where's Alice?"

"She was over by that piece of statuary just a minute ago, Jim. She was with Lucy and Rick. I'm sure she's close. Ah, see, here come Lucy and Rick now," Karen assured as Rick came around a corner, his striking seventeen-year-old sister in tow.

"Rick, where's Alice? Mom said she was with you."

"Nope—must be with Johanna. We just stopped to look at the elephant painting again. Lucy just can't get over how cute it looks!" he mocked as he smiled at his younger sister.

"Not with me!" Johanna piped up as she stepped out from

behind her mother.

"Jim?" Karen's motherly instincts kicked in. Turning to the children she demanded, "When was the last time any of you saw Alice?"

And that's when Jim first felt the magic of the place that was to enter their lives, for although he could hear their three older children stammer in self-defense, a calm unlike anything he had ever felt before enveloped him, not unlike the robes worn by the monks that still inhabited Angkor Wat—comfortable, warm, and just a little mysterious.

Without saying a word, Jim reached over and took his wife's hand, motioning with a nod of his head to follow. Though he had no idea where he was going, he knew exactly where they were headed. They were going to find Alice.

Jim and Karen quickly retraced their steps about thirty feet back down the hall, then felt drawn to turn right, even though they had come from the left. There, fifteen feet away and chatting with an older man was little Alice, as comfortable as young Jesus must have been with the learned men on the steps of the Jerusalem Temple. Though the Callisters had never seen this man before, they both felt immediately that she was in no danger; in silence they stood back and watched the scene before them.

The older man was not kneeling in a western position but rather squatted comfortably as he gazed eye to eye with their daughter. Extracting something from a pocket in his robes, he pressed it into her hands, whispering warmly as he did so. Karen could not resist and raised her camera to capture the moment. An unusual feeling of gratitude washed over her just as she pressed the button— warm light from the late afternoon sun flooded her subjects through a lower window as her viewfinder revealed an image normally reserved for the front cover of *National Geographic.* With or without the picture, Jim and Karen would never forget that moment.

The flash seemed to alert the old man that he had visitors. He looked over at Karen and Jim—and their children, who had caught up to them and had been equally captivated by the scene—and immediately recognized the situation. A concerned family had come looking for their precious missing one. He smiled warmly at the little troupe, and they knew that Alice had been in no danger. Then turning back to Alice, he clasped her little hands in his own, tapped at whatever he had given her, and whispered gently. At that, he rose and shuffled off down the hall.

"Alice, who was that?" Johanna blurted out, now that the magic of the moment had gone with the disappearance of the old man. "What did he give you?"

"And why didn't you tell us where you were?" chastised the ever-protective Rick.

Alice gave her family the look that all nine-year-old girls seem to know instinctively, the one that says, *I knew exactly where I was this whole time. Don't get all huffy! There was nothing to worry about!* Walking up to her mother, she opened up her hand and said, "He gave me this bracelet. Isn't it pretty?"

Karen looked at the gift with a practiced eye—and was nearly mesmerized. It was simultaneously simple and elegant, bearing no precious stones yet somehow invaluable. Light blue stones were bound loosely together on a leather string—it reminded Karen of the old man himself: a simple exterior that belied the power that surged just under the surface. She reached out to finger the stones and sensed a warmth and peace deep in her heart as she did so. There was definitely something magical about this sacred temple!

Jim heard a step behind him and turned to see that Tree had joined them. "Did you see this older man, Tree? Do you know him?"

"I am sorry, Mr. Callister. I have never seen him before, although he walks as if he is comfortable with these surroundings. If that is the case, it is strange, for I give tours here regularly, and yet I have never seen him."

"His robes—they did not seem to be the same as the robes of other monks we have seen today. Do they mean anything to you?"

"Again I am sorry, Mr. Callister. They were unlike anything worn by our local monks, and yet I must admit that there was something hauntingly familiar about them, as if I should know them by sight and know of their considerable meaning. Very strange, I must say.

"One more thing that you should know, Mr. Callister. I

overheard just a bit of what he was whispering to your little one. He was speaking a blessing, the words of which are very ancient and very sacred. Few outside this temple know this blessing. I only came across it last fall as I was browsing the archives looking for descriptions of how the temple was built. I found an old but very well preserved text that spoke of an unusual spirit that attended this most famous of all temples, a spirit that connected this world with the world of those who had passed on before. The bracelet that he gave your daughter contains very old symbols that remind one of this blessing and its meaning."

Though much of what the guide had said escaped Alice's understanding, she understood enough to know that this was a very unusual gift. But then, that was something that she already grasped as soon as the old man had wrapped his worn fingers around her young ones and pressed the bracelet tight against the palm of her right hand. As she looked up into her mother's deep blue eyes, she smiled, then radiated the afternoon light in her smile. Somehow they both knew that she would never be the same after this day.

Part Two: Angels

Chapter 18

"Mom!" Fourteen-year-old Alice called down the stairs from her bedroom. "Have you seen my bracelet?"

"You've got several pieces of jewelry on the kitchen table, honey, along with several other items that you left here when you got home from the movie last evening. I'm not sure if one of them is a bracelet or not, but I'll bet if you put them away you'd be able to tell." Karen shook her head gently and smiled. Alice was the last of her children to pass through being a teenager, and every one went through the same stage of using the entire house as a combination dressing room, storage closet, and dining room. And every one had also been the recipient of frequent reminders to pick things up, put them away, turn lights off, and replace items into the refrigerator.

"No, Mom, not *that* bracelet! I mean *the* bracelet! *My* bracelet! The one I got from the old monk in Cambodia! Seen it anywhere?"

"Oh, *that* bracelet! Alice, I'm sorry, but I haven't seen you wear that bracelet for years. Where do you usually keep it?" She knew that usually keeping anything in an organized place was pushing the limits for the age, but Karen also knew just how much that bracelet had meant to her daughter. And knowing that, Karen decided that this was one of those times when a mother should help her daughter, so thirty seconds later she had ascended the stairs and stood in Alice's doorway.

"Any luck? I truly haven't seen it for a long time, munchkin, but what's the occasion? What made you think of it now, after so long?"

"At dinner, you started talking about Grandma and all the service she's done over the years. I thought about the dozens and dozens of quilts that she and her friends put together when we went to Cambodia, and how hard it was to fit them all into our luggage and extra bags—boy, it's sure good that we didn't have to pay for each piece of luggage then like we do now! We would never have made it nowdays! Anyway, thinking about Grandma's quilts made me think of how grateful those kids were in the hospital to be able to wrap up in them when they were nothing but skin and bones and on the verge of death.

"You taught us a lot about service on that trip, Mom. I'm very proud of you!" Alice paused to beam at her mother, and then turned back to her dresser top. "But thinking about that trip also made me think of talking to that old monk in the temple on our last day. Remember how safe I felt, even though I had wandered away from the rest of the family, and how he gave me that old-fashioned bracelet? It's hard to describe, Mom, and you'll probably think I'm a bit strange, but that bracelet almost seemed to have some sort of extra powers or something. I always felt safe when I wore it, but then I got into more modern fashions and the bracelet didn't quite measure up anymore.

"I think it's time to bring that old bracelet out of storage, Mom, but it's not where I keep it. What do I do?"

No sooner had the words left her mouth when Alice's cell phone started singing to her. She glanced quickly at the text that had just been announced and turned to her mother in yet another teenage panic. "Oh, no! Mom, I told Sue I'd help her study for her physics test tomorrow. She's outside with her mom waiting to pick me up right now. Can we look for this later?"

Karen just smiled, "Of course, Alice. Wherever your bracelet has gotten off to, chances are it won't stray very far while you're studying with Sue. Besides, I promised Grandma that I'd come over this evening to help her sort through her financial papers. We'll look another time."

"Thanks, Mom! You're the greatest ever!" And off she bounced—out of her bedroom, down the stairs, and right out the front door.

Four hours later Alice came back in through the front door the same way she left—with energy. Yes, she had had a good study session. No, Sue didn't have any boys over (other than that fine-looking older brother of hers!). Yes, they did listen to some music while studying—especially after they were done. Sue had just downloaded a new CD onto her I-Pod, and it was smokin' hot! She and Sue had closed the door to her bedroom and danced like silly little girls, danced until they collapsed on the bed, and then laughed the giddy laugh of exhausted dancer-scholars who had accomplished much. But now it was time to get ready for bed and a good night's rest!

After kissing her parents good-night, a ritual that had started years ago and that none of them wanted to outgrow just yet, she trotted up the stairs, brushed her teeth, and got ready for bed. After climbing into bed, she leaned over to shut off the light on her nightstand when she noticed something sticking out from under her pillow—the frayed end of her bracelet! "Oh, Mom came through yet again! She must have found it and put it here for me to see." Alice slipped the trinket over her wrist and smiled as a familiar peace settled over her. "I think I'm going to sleep well tonight."

Most dreams are a meaningless freeflow of random thoughts and impulses. They are a composite of half-finished conversations, various images seen throughout the day, and the chemical reaction of stomach acids and whatever went down the ol' pipes during various meals and snack times. Such dreams should be ignored and forgotten.

Some dreams are important, and their meaning can be unearthed by using classic dream interpretation theory. Various parts of a person's persona are played out symbolically by parents, friends, teachers, and the like. If correctly viewed and not misunderstood by thinking that the people in the dream actually represent themselves, powerful insights into the dreamer's mind can be gained. Such dreams should be remembered and investigated, perhaps even reexamined from time to time.

And then there is that other class of dream, the one in which reality really does blend with the unseen in an uncanny revelatory experience. Call them mystical, inspirational, or weird, they offer to the dreamer a life-changing experience in which the supernatural and the natural mingle freely for a time. Some people seem to be more open to such experiences, while others seem appointed to have them despite a total lack of spiritual sensitivity. Alice was one of the former, though until now she was largely unaware of her gift. But shortly after midnight, that all changed—even though she never left her bed and her eyes never opened, she was more aware of the experience than anything she had ever encountered before.

"Oh, hello. I remember you . . . I think. You're the monk from Angkor Wat who found me when I wandered away from my family, right? What are you doing here?" They were seated comfortably in the family room of the Callister family home, Alice on the couch and the old man facing her from her dad's favorite leather reading chair. She was vaguely aware that this was an unusual setting, yet everything seemed so comfortable and familiar and . . . right.

"My dear Alice. You have grown so beautiful. Only a very good heart can produce such beauty, you know. But yes, you asked who I am. I am what you might call a guardian angel. I am near you mostly at two occasions—when you need my help, and when you are giving help to others. You remember me from when we met in the sacred temple in Cambodia. I was able to visit you then because of your purity and your service."

"Service?"

"Oh, yes. There are many in the world who cry out for assistance to get through their challenges. Far fewer respond by reaching out to assist with goodness and true mercy. A donation of money can provide great service, it is true, but mercy requires a donation of the heart as well. Only those who understand both can create lasting goodness for others. Alice, you must understand that when your mother planned your family trip to Cambodia, she was assisted by many of my fellow guardian angels who knew the good that would be done by your family's involvement. Will you do me a favor? Sit down with your mother, and help her to realize how many doors were opened to help her plan the trip. Help her understand the guardian angels whom she assisted by being open to their whispered influence."

"Is that why you are visiting me now? To help my mother understand the value of her gifts to others a decade ago?"

"That is where we must start, Alice. You see, little one, you have a special gift, a unique gift. I know of no other mortal now alive who is open as you are to our communication, but we must learn to trust each other. Soon I will be able to give you some very direct advice."

"Advice about what?"

"In time, Alice, all in good time. For now, it is enough for you to visit with your mother. Wear your bracelet, and I will help you know what to say." The monk stood as if to leave.

"Please don't leave yet! I don't understand!" exclaimed Alice, reaching out and grasping his arm by the loose sleeve of his robe.

The old man sighed a sigh that any parent would recognize. It was the sigh of submission and acknowledgment that he was going to be here awhile yet. He sat on the edge of the couch and turned so as to mostly face his young student. "Alice, think of it in this way. Everyone on the earth is blessed with an inner compass that leads us to what is right. Some call that compass the heart, science calls it a conscience, others think of it as a feeling. I believe your own faith refers to it as the light of Christ. Regardless of what we call this inner compass, it exists in every person. Some listen to its direction, others may only be innocently aware of a feeling now and then, and still others ignore its guidance altogether. But know this, little one, it is very real! Through understanding and experience, everyone can learn to rely on the quiet influence in order to live a better life."

Alice was intrigued—after all, she was talking to an old monk in her family room in the middle of the night as if it were the most natural thing in the world to be doing! "But I don't get it! I mean, yes, I understand what you said, and I recognize the feelings that you spoke of. But why are you here now? In my house? You have to admit, my friends would probably accuse me of taking up drugs if I were to tell them what's going on here."

"Ah, yes. You know, I'm a little bit rusty at this myself. I haven't really had a chance to speak with a mortal since I chatted with a lost little girl in a temple in Cambodia. It seems like yesterday to me, but, well, anyway, back to your question. This spirit that I told you of is only part of your personal guidance system. There are many who have already passed from mortality—people like me, for example—and many who will yet be born who have a deep interest in your well being and want to see you accomplish many great things. In your life, you may elect to get married and have children, or you may put into motion some other action that will make a difference to those yet to come. There are many unseen individuals who care very much for you and about what you do."

"There are? I mean, I think I've always believed in some sort of connection between my ancestors and me, and I sometimes daydream about the children I will someday have. Sometimes I think that somehow I already know them. But as far as I know, we don't have any Cambodian relatives, and you don't exactly look like a red-headed Viking. No offense, but how do you figure into my life?"

"That's a good question, Alice. You're right, I am from Cambodia, as were my ancestors and my children and children's children. But time and space are not so limiting in my world as they are in yours. Let's try something. In the morning, visit with your mother. Ask her what obstacles she encountered in planning your trip, and then have her tell you how she overcame them."

"I will, but that doesn't answer my question. How do you figure into our lives?"

The old monk smiled at his young friend's persistence. It was a trait that would bless not only her life but many others in the years to come. "Okay, Alice, you win! Do you remember the young girl in the hospital that you helped to paint? She was dying with AIDS and did not have much longer to live?"

"Yes, I do. That was very sad for me. I was so little and didn't understand much about either AIDS or death, and I certainly couldn't see why someone so young should have to die."

The monk's voice grew yet softer and more tender, if that were possible: "That little girl was my granddaughter. She lived a very short and difficult life, and she never really felt the love of another human being. When she was born, my daughter was very poor and had been making a living selling herself on the streets. She had so few options. She tried so hard to care for her little one, but it was just too much. When she was three, she left her in front of a Christian church one morning. The priest took her to the appropriate officials, who suspected the truth and had her tested for AIDS. The test was positive, so they immediately took her to the hospital where you saw her. They had no other options.

"It broke my heart to watch my granddaughter alone and dying, and I couldn't do a thing to help her. But then I became aware of your family's intention to come to Cambodia. I learned of the tremendous influence for good that you all could provide, so I assisted in small ways to ensure that you could make the trip and come to the hospital in safety. Your mother will be aware of those times.

"I was at the hospital when your family arrived. The love you gave to my precious little one that day has carried with her into the next life. I cannot begin to tell you how much that meant to me to know that she had finally experience love!" Tears filled the old man's eyes. "Bet you didn't know that angels can cry, now did you?"

"But that was not all, Alice. My granddaughter spent her final hours in that little room that your family painted. It brought her great peace and joy because of the characters on the wall and the joy with which they were painted. That room has been touched up several times since you were in Phnom Penh, but the painters are always careful to keep the original images just as they were done. The paint can be refreshed, but the original love can never be improved on. That room has comforted and provided joy and peace to literally hundreds of children in their final hours since your visit.

"And there is more. The doctor who oversaw the hospital would have quit the next day if your family had not come. She felt she was not making a difference and had told her husband of her desire to leave the facility. She had lost sight of the great good that she was doing. But your mother told her woman to woman in a way that she could really understand that she was so blessed to be in a position to help so many people who needed help so desperately. There was truly no one else in that part of the world who could improve the lives of those people in the way she did. If she weren't doing what she was doing, hundreds would suffer more than they were.

"As she walked through the open market with you, she saw so many people whose lives she had improved or even saved. Many acknowledged her with merely a gesture, a nod of the head, a wave of recognition, but every one of them conveyed to her in their way a sincere gratitude for what she had done. When she returned to the hospital, she had decided to stay. Your mother's influence convinced her to stay and save hundreds more over the years. If Karen Callister had not listened to the quiet influences directing her to Cambodia, who knows what would have happened. Many, many guardian angels helped to ensure that your mother could overcome the roadblocks that came up in her travel plans!

"Your father set in motion a series of events that will forever change the lives of many people in my home country. Do you recall when he refused to allow Tree to stay in a boarding house and was eventually able to convince the hotel manager to let Tree stay in your brother's room?"

"Sure. We all loved Tree. He was so kind to me especially. I still send him cards from time to time!"

"Ah, yes, I had nearly forgotten about the cards. I'm so glad that you do that. But Tree is such a humble man that I doubt you know all of what he has done with his life since serving as your driver, translator, and guide a decade ago. He was so impressed with what your family did for him that he gained much confidence and desire to improve life for others. Two years after you returned to your home, he sought and won an election to a public position where he can put into position actions against the mistreatment of lower classes. It will take time to overcome thousands of years of unjust prejudice, but he found in his interaction with your family a passion to serve. Because of your family's example of love, dedication, and tenacity, he has taught many others to live out their dreams. This contact with Tree and your family came with the assistance of many angels from all over the world.

"Are you beginning to see that your family's trip meant far more than just a vacation to an interesting place?"

"Yes, I am, although it seems that my presence there was of no consequence."

"Be patient, little one, and you will see. For your role is not yet finished. But first, you will remember your brother's friend at the orphanage? He had lost his desire to live, Alice. When Rick acknowledged this boy and talked to his soul by showing him unconditional love the young man renewed his interest in life. He has gone on to be a leader among the kids at the orphanage and has helped many of them find homes with good families. Rick's kindess that day preserved a young man's life, which has lead to a tidal wave of positive movement toward the spirits of those who have lived there, are living there now, and will yet live there.

"At the second orphanage your family visited, your sister inspired two young ladies to express themselves in art. They have since been recognized for their art, and as a result one is attending college on scholarship and the other gives all her painting proceeds to those who are orphaned.

"The young man your other sister acknowledged and teased in the village gained self-confidence from his playing with her. I'm sure she could never have imagined that her sensitivity in how she handled that young man could mean so much to his life. He has become a social and technological leader in the village and promotes self-reliance, which is what your family taught them that day.

"You see, Alice, small acts of kindness ripple across the great oceans of need when love is expressed and used to provide assistance; those ripples later become positive tidal waves. We on this side understand the need and do all in our power to persuade our mortal counterparts to help for we are so limited in what we are actually allowed to do. I shudder to think what may not have happened if for some reason your mother had given up and chosen Disney World over Cambodia.

"And now our time is up, my dear friend Alice. You must sleep. But please don't forget to visit with your mother—find out how she felt so strongly about your family making this trip, and share with her the success of your visit." And with that he was gone.

Chapter 19

"Alice! Time to wake up, honey!" Karen Callister was never one to let her children sleep in on a school day. Surprisingly, Alice popped right up this morning, looking as if she were coming out of the most restful sleep of her young life.

"Hey, Mom. Thanks for waking me. Got a minute?"

"Sure. What's up?"

"Thanks for finding my bracelet and putting it under my pillow where I could see it! That was way sweet of you!"

"Oh, Alice, I completely forgot about looking for it last night. I went over to help Grandma, and when I got back it slipped my mind. But there it is on your wrist. Did you really find it under your pillow?"

"Yeah. Strange, huh? But that wasn't the strangest thing that happened last night. I'd like to tell you about a dream I had if you've got a few minutes."

"Sure. I think we have time for a little mother-daughter chat before you need to get ready for school." Karen came through the bedroom doorway and sat comfortably on the end of her daughter's bed. "So, tell me about this dream. Any boys involved?" she teased.

"I suppose you could say so, if boys includes a very old man! Do you remember the old monk who gave me this bracelet in Angkor Wat?"

"Of course. I will never forget how scared we were when we noticed you were gone, and then how completely peaceful we felt when we saw the two of you together. He was an unusual man, wasn't he! Is that what you dreamed about?"

"Sort of. I mean, yes, it was all about him, but it was almost more than a dream, if that can make sense. I could almost swear that he was right here in the house, and we were having a conversation down in the family room. Anyway, I can still remember everything about it. We talked about how we all have feelings in our hearts about what is right and that as we learn to follow those feelings we become better at understanding."

"Well, I certainly agree with that, Alice. You know we've talked about that as a family many times."

"I know, but I've never heard it from a dead monk in a dream before!"

"Well, you've got me there," Karen laughed. "What else did you talk about? It sounds as if this was a very important dream if you remember it so clearly."

"I think so, Mom. It wasn't like any dream I've ever had before. He talked about people who are yet to come into our lives and those who have gone on before. He said that some of them become what he called guardian angels. He said that they do everything they can to help us in small ways to understand and appreciate life while we are here in mortality."

"Did he say he was your guardian angel?" Karen remembered how she felt in meeting him and thought of the positive reaction many had when they saw the picture of him giving Alice the bracelet. So many had commented that there was something about that picture that soothed the soul. Karen had long felt that her ancestors still had an influence on her somehow, and there was no getting around the feeling that Alice and the old monk seemed to have some sort of bond.

"No, not mine. I had wondered that myself, as it would have explained why I felt so connected to him when he gave me the bracelet. But maybe he is for one of the people we met in Cambodia. He said in their world it is just as important to help those who will help the people they watch over, and he knew what we could do."

"What did you do for him?"

"Well, it wasn't just me, but remember the little girl in the hospital who was dying—the one I fell in love with? He said that was his granddaughter. He told me that I was able to show her love in her last days, something that she knew very little of. That one experience made her last days tolerable, happy, and fulfilled. He feels that is why he was given permission to meet me at the temple, because I had helped his granddaughter die happy." Alice's eyes welled up with tender tears at the memory of the little girl.

"Alice, I don't really know what happened last night, but something in my heart is telling me that this man is very special and that this was not just a dream. I don't know what to call it, but I sense that it was something unusual and very important."

"Oh, Mom, thanks for not laughing at me or calling me weird or something. I know it sounds bizarre, but it was all so very real to me. He also said some things about you." Karen's eyebrows went up in interest as Alice continued. "He said that your desires to take our family on that trip were supported by many on the other side who knew what good we would do in the lives of those we met. When I told him of the good we gained as a family and how it changed our lives, he said that our guardians knew and helped as well. He asked me to ask you about your experiences, especially working through the roadblocks that came up in your planning."

"You know, Alice, this puts a very different light on the whole thing for me. I mean, from the very first time that I had an impression to have some experience in serving as a family, I knew that I needed to follow through with that impression. But it wasn't always easy. There were times when I almost gave up, but each time I was ready to give into the road blocks, I would pray for help. There was always an intervention of some kind to motivate me to continue. I had always thought that the trip was important for what we would learn, but you're telling me that the service we gave made a difference in Cambodia as well!"

Alice excitedly shared what the messenger had told him about the good they had done and what had happened in the intervening years. "Mom, he said that many on the other side were there to ensure that we could go to Cambodia and do so safely. But I have a question. He told me of the good things that we were able to do, but what do you think we learned?"

"Well, Alice, think about these things and see if you agree with me. The biggest lesson that I learned is that happiness comes from deep within. The world concentrates on material things, which distracts us from finding contentment. I have found that reflecting on the blessings of having a family, friends, good health, knowledge, hope, and love bring me far more pleasure and satisfaction than merely owning stuff.

"I was also impressed by the Cambodian belief that those who come to this world with deformities are blessings from our Creator to the families they live with. They are trusted to those who are capable of helping them, and the process of participating in their lives hallows those who help as nothing else can.

"I remember speaking with Tree about their beliefs regarding love and romance. For them, falling in love consists more in finding common interests and ideals, and then working together to accomplish those interests. Satisfying physical desires before marriage only clouds the mind in finding cherished soul mates. Sexual relations are a part of marriage, not physical desire alone.

"The last one that comes to mind right now is perhaps more of a personal lesson for me. Every time I perceived a setback or roadblock, I was also presented with an opportunity to grow, learn, or act in a new way. We need never lose hope as long as we remember to look for the opportunities presented in each challenge.

"Alice, many times I prayed, and each time I tried to remember to offer gratitude for small gifts of support. Each time I gained a stronger commitment as my heart began to swell with conviction. You might not know this, but I kept a diary about that whole experience. When you get home from school, let's go through it together, and I will show you what I wrote."

"Really, Mom? That sounds so cool! I can hardly wait. Mom, I know this sounds odd, but do you think he will visit me again?"

"Did he tell you he would?" Karen asked gently.

"Not really, but for some reason I'm pretty sure I still have something to learn from him. It's just a feeling, but—and I know this sounds weird—but wearing this bracelet seems to make me think a bit better and see more clearly. I think I will wear it for a while."

Chapter 20

"Hello, Alice. It's so nice to see you again."

It had been just over two weeks since she had dreamed of the old monk. In those weeks, Alice and her parents had had several lengthy discussions about her dream and what she had learned. Curiosity had gotten the best of Jim, and he had contacted Mike, who was still coordinating humanitarian efforts in Phnom Penh for private American charities. Jim casually asked about Tree and the doctor at the hospital for the dying. "Oh, you would no longer recognize your friend Tree, Jim. He left me about five years ago to become an elected official and is doing so many wonderful things to overcome the class system here. He speaks of your family every time I see him. And our doctor continues to work miracles. I don't know how she does it. She is just magnificent."

For some reason, Jim was not surprised. Neither were the rest of the family members when he reported what Mike had said, Alice least of all. One evening the whole family got together and looked at their pictures of the trip to Cambodia. They laughed a lot, cried now and then, and shared many, many feelings and impressions.

They also talked long into the night about the events that had transpired since their trip—hard times, good times, learning times. Alice contributed from time to time, but mostly she listened and remembered. Although she was naturally a bright young lady, on this evening she seemed to have a heightened sense of being able to remember what each member of the family shared, cataloging each story into a mental folder labeled "Cambodia."

And now the old man was back. Or rather, she was back, for this time the scenario was not her family room downstairs but instead the sacred temple of Angkor Wat. They stood at the very place they had been when they first met.

"Hello! I was wondering if I would ever see you again."

"Those who oversee my efforts as a guardian angel wanted to make sure that you responded correctly to my visit. Not everyone can handle knowing they had a visit from the other side, you know," he said as his eyes twinkled. "But they have given me permission to see you again in order to give you a most precious gift."

"But how could there be anything more precious than the bracelet that you gave me, well, the last time I was here in the temple? Though humble, it is my most prized possession."

"Do you remember that when I slipped the bracelet on your wrist, I spoke to you words that you did not understand? I marveled at the time that you did not ask me what I was saying. It was as if you understood the sacred nature of my blessing without knowing the specifics."

Alice bowed her head and almost whispered, "In all the years since that time, I have spoken to no one of that moment, old friend. I have discussed the bracelet and how special it is to me, but the feelings that came over me when you spoke words that I did not know were indeed sacred. I have never felt that I could share that moment with anyone, not even my parents. What is it that you said? Can I know now?"

"Dear Alice, do you have any idea just how special you are? Of course you don't—that's part of what makes you who you are. The words that accompanied my gift of the bracelet were part of an ancient covenant blessing. The language was Sanskrit, the oldest known language on the earth today. Few know the sound of the language and how to speak it. Like the bracelet, the blessing may seem common, but the power that attends those words will change your life. I have been given permission to bring you to this ancient temple today to teach you the words in your own language. As special as your home is to you, there are some things that can only be taught in places where heaven and earth meet in a divine column that reaches from the natural to the supernatural and back again. This temple is one of those places. You will find others as you go through your life, but this is one that I have access to and that is home to the blessing of the bracelet.

"I will give you the ten values of the bracelet. You must then commit them to memory. It is very important that you remember and apply them. Listen well, my little one. I will tell them to you once, but that will be enough. Write them in your journal, and later we will find ways to teach you the principles associated with the ten values in greater detail." With that, the old monk touched his fingertips lightly to the temples of his guest. Alice closed her eyes, and when she opened them again, he was gone.

∞ ∞ ∞

When Alice awoke, it was Saturday morning. The sun was shining, and birds chirped merrily outside her bedroom window. On the nightstand next to the bed lay a new maroon journal and a new blue pen, her favorite colors.

She picked them up, held them briefly to her heart, said a quiet prayer, and began writing:

Honesty
Generosity
Patience
Virtue
Kindness
Equanimity
Discernment
Wisdom
Courage
Determination

Alice felt that the ten values she had learned came unusually easy for her to remember and sat marveling at each of the ten words that she had written. A calm peace overcame her as she subconsciously reached over and picked up the bracelet.

What happened next can only be explained by those who have had similar experiences in life. Alice felt a burning in her bosom, a complete sense of peace, and she felt as though time had no boundaries. *Could it be that the window to heaven has opened and I am near?*

Alice felt as if her mortality were just a blip on the radar of life—as if her life were part of some divine, even eternal, plan and was somehow intended to test her faith. Her right to choose her life's path was guaranteed by natural law. She began to cry with joy, knowing that her heart was the compass that enabled her to make correct decisions. She knew with an unexplainable certainty that her life was a progression towards perfection.

The words that her friend had given her were character traits that if lived would enable tremendous growth. She knew that if she were able to master them, life would be precious indeed and allow her to help others to experience the same fulfillment and joy.

She looked at the list she had written—it was as if the words came alive, and without thought the ancient sayings her friend had spoken provided incredible understanding and meaning. Not wanting to miss anything, Alice picked her pen up and wrote:

- *Honesty: Be sincere in relationships. Speaking with integrity builds bonds. Master being genuine in candor, for this will comfort others who will understand your intent.*

- *Generosity: Value the spirit of giving. Obtaining the knowledge that resources in this abundant world are plentiful to those who share will serve you well.*

- *Patience: Nature, by example, shows us that our personal development comes over time. Anything worthwhile grows methodically, building on a strong foundation. Develop a willingness to carry on despite roadblocks.*

- *Virtue: Purity in thought and deed builds lasting relationships—with the support of loved ones, nothing can destroy you.*

- *Kindness: Show empathy and charity to all. Seeing others from their perspective will open your mind. Observe, knowing that it is more important to understand what others sense than to dwell on how you feel.*

- *Equanimity: Maintain composure in times of heightened emotion. React only when your thoughts are calm and clear. Being sensible will open doors for solutions and creativity.*

- *Discernment: The natural being, left free to explore untamed, will lead to devastation. Learn to restrain unrighteous physical desires. Those desires, applied in moderation in proper times and places, can fill your soul with happiness.*

• *Wisdom: The ability to understand and reason will prove invaluable. Wisdom navigates paths of success, allowing you to accomplish anything. It is not necessary to live through all of life's available experiences in order to gain wisdom—many have already learned by practice and will teach you willingly.*

• *Courage: Maintain a willing spirit in all you do. The mind functions in such a way that whatever is thought is lived. Build strength and vitality in life, and the energy will carry you to greatness.*

• *Determination: Have an unyielding will, manifest in boldness and perseverance. Know in your heart that when you have committed, nothing will stop you.*

Exhausted by the intensity of the spirit that immersed Alice in its light and understanding, she lay her head on the desk, weakened but peaceful.

Waking a few hours later, she lifted her head and began reading the notes she had written earlier in her journal. There's no way that I wrote this! I'm only fourteen, and this is stuff that I'd expect to find in Rick's college philosophy books. The wisdom contained in these words is amazing!

Her guardian angel had suggested that he would share some simple life lessons that would bring greater understanding, but this was something else. This was nearly visionary! Alice could hardly wait until her angel friend would return and begin teaching her more.

Part Three: Lessons

Be sincere in relationships; speaking with integrity builds bonds. Master being genuine in candor—this will comfort others who will understand our intent.

Chapter 21

"Guardian Angel, something has been on my mind, but I'm not sure whether I should bother you with it."

"Little one, I can't think of anything in this world that you can't ask me about. I might not answer the way you want, but you can always ask."

"Mom told me the other day about a man whom she has admired for years. He was successful, outgoing, and well liked, but Mom just found out that he had been having an affair for many years with his secretary, and most of his business success was the result of stealing the intellectual property of his former business partner. His apparent success had come at the price of his former partner, whose career was permanently damaged; his secretary's reputation, who will never be the same; and more important his wife and family, whom he should have loved and protected above everyone else in life. How can someone do that? And what about those who don't get caught, as this man wasn't for many years?"

"Hypocrisy and deceit are sometimes difficult to detect, aren't they? Sometimes they can be hidden for significant periods of time, but wrongdoing cannot be masked forever.

"Think of a large, deep lake high in the mountains. During the winter, it is covered with a sheet of ice. Trust is like that ice. When we begin our lives, everyone is gifted a sufficient thickness of ice to allow others to believe in us. We can carry the weight of their belief without threat of breaking through.

"Imagine that someone is willing to venture out with you on a thickness of six inches of ice. You stand on it over hundreds of feet of freezing water, water that would take your life within seconds if you fell in. Distance from the shore doesn't really matter with ice—when the temperature is constant and cold enough, the thickness supports weight along any point over the water.

"As our life begins, we can bear the weight of responsibility for most situations. When we show trust to others, we begin to build the thickness of our ice. Over time, as we consistently present honesty and truth to those around us, our ice grows until we can bear nearly any weight that can be placed on us. Others see our goodness and build our strength by validating our honor.

"If, however, we find ourselves falling away from truth, our ice begins to melt. At first, the minor change in thickness doesn't matter. The danger lies mostly in the trend towards dishonesty, and if we don't see any negative consequences in lying, we can easily fall into the trap of finding excuses for not telling the truth. We tell more and more, and soon there are various places on the ice that no longer support as they should. Water begins to appear through the cracks, and very quickly we have no support for anyone to join with us.

"Alice, as you go through your life you will witness many who have been given, assumed, or chosen a role of leadership. The diversity of leadership positions can be as intimate as a parent-child relationship or as broad as the leadership of a country. Many leaders whom we observe possess an ability to move us to tremendous achievements—they create in us a desire to serve.

"Other leaders have styles that lack the ability to stir us toward common good because no one will walk out on the ice with them. These ineffective leaders are incapable of finding true followers or believers because they are not true to their position.

"A true leader in any position performs without seeking or aspiring to that place for the honor of mankind, but does so to better an individual, a group, or the world.

"We want our leaders to be confident and have high self-regard—they are our mentors. We want to emulate true leaders. They teach us about the greatness we have inside, they promote our own abilities, and they allow us to be better for having known them. Tests of one's ability to lead include how much respect is earned from those whom they lead, a measure of the fruits of their, service, and continued admiration after the title is gone.

"Your recent discussion with your mother has already identified the results of dishonesty in one who should have known better and performed far more honorably. Be wary of those who cloak their actions and discussions in secrecy without a need to do so, for they are hiding something. Trust those who openly disclose their history and the reasons for their actions and who are willing to walk on the ice with you."

With that, her angel departed, and Alice turned to her journal as she always did. At the end of her entry, she wrote:

Happiness comes by experiencing both good and bad times. My sharing life experiences honestly allows for others to find joy.

I am honest.

We must value the spirit of giving; obtaining knowledge we live in an abundant world and that resources are plentiful will serve us well. Compassion for selfless service ensures we will never want.

Chapter 22

On the Wednesday following her guardian angel's lesson on honesty, Alice began to learn. She belonged to a youth group that met each Wednesday evening to seek out learning and service opportunities. Sometimes they would visit a place of business in a field of interest to several of the girls, but more often than not they looked for opportunities to serve others in simple ways. Just last week they had visited an aging care facility, and the week before that they had made chocolate chip cookies for a new family who had just moved into the neighborhood.

This evening Alice had arranged for their group to hold a "movie night" for some of the children at the local children's hospital. The hospital had a large meeting room that could accommodate about 50 people, so Alice arranged for a recent Disney movie, a projector, and a large screen, and the hospital allowed 45 of their more mobile patients to come in and watch. The remaining places were taken by Alice's youth group and a half dozen nurses to ensure the children were in good hands. Ever since the Callisters had visited the AIDS hospital on their first day in Cambodia, Alice had had a tender place in her heart for sick children who just needed a little cheer and brightness in their lives.

And now, at the end of the day, Alice was sitting down to record the events of the evening in her new journal before turning in for the night. Suddenly she felt someone peering over her shoulder, but not in an eerie frightening sort of way. No, this was more like an old friend, so she ventured a guess: "Guardian Angel, is that you?" And turning in her seat, she was pleased to see his familiar form standing three paces behind her left shoulder.

"You're getting very hard to sneak up on, Alice. That pleases me, although I admit I enjoyed the surprised look on your face from time to time."

"You probably already know this, but I was just writing in my journal about going to the children's hospital this evening. It was a simple thing that we did, but those children seemed to appreciate it so much. I forget that they really don't have much entertainment in their lives."

"Alice, your experience in the hospital is just what I wanted to build on tonight as I teach you the value of generosity, a principle associated with the bracelet. Alice, we are taught that it is better to give than receive. Do you know what this really means? Do you really understand the abundance of the world?

"When you give of your abundance, you gain a deep love of your fellow beings, an intense understanding of life, and—this one might surprise you—an ability to move through personal crisis by giving. When your family went across the world to provide service to a country with people in great need, you were still quite young. This trip, from a worldly perspective, cost a great deal of money. Some of your parents' friends tried to talk them out of going, suggesting that the experience would simply 'not be worth it.' Many people thought that there were many other things that they should do before expending the time, effort, and money to do what your family did. But as it turned out, more lives than you can imagine were changed from the experience—including each member of your family from the adults to the youngest." The old man's eyes twinkled knowingly as he winked at Alice.

"All the money in the world wouldn't have given you the experience and education that you received from your adventure. You now know there is a big world out there and not all have been given the same opportunities. You have great sympathy for the less privileged and your desire to help is evidenced by your quiet actions, such as what you and your friends did at the children's hospital this evening.

"Your understanding of how easily one person can alter the course of another's life has been permanently enhanced. You are now unafraid to offer help, ideas, or assistance because you know firsthand the miracles that can come from a simple action. No college could give you this kind of education in a classroom. No talk could have inspired greater convictions. No reading could have solidified a deeper, more intense or sincere love for others.

"Now, Alice, I have been given permission to show you something very special. Take my hand and tell me what you see."

"Wow! I had nearly forgotten what it feels like to touch you, but now it all comes back to me. I remember such comfort when I was lost in the temple and you found me. I felt peaceful, safe, and like I understood things that I never understood before. And now? This is just like that Christmas show with Ebenezer Scrooge. I see a young man whom I don't recognize. How can I see him, and who is this boy?"

"Time and space have different boundaries in my world, Alice. I have received permission to share this ability with you when I hold your hand so you can learn more quickly. The young man you see here has been blessed today to have those who love him intercede at a critical time. What do you think of his mood, of his emotional state?"

"Oh, this kid is on a major downer! His face looks tortured, and his eyes are so dark! But maybe because he's carrying two backpacks and two boxes as well. What is he carrying?"

"Alice, this boy is very sad. He has lost all sense of who he is—I mean really is—and thinks that he is just a burden to everyone who knows him. He can no longer see that he has value in his world. Because he doesn't want to be a burden any longer, he went to school earlier today and cleaned out his locker so no one would have to do it after he is gone. He is walking home, where he plans to take his life this afternoon, and has a lot to carry, physically and emotionally. Let's see if we can help him, shall we?" With that, the monk reached his free hand forward as if he were pushing something away.

Suddenly the top box shifted in the boy's arms and slid from its perch atop the other box. The boy shifted his load quickly and tried to regain control, but he only succeeded in overcorrecting, and the box went tumbling to the ground. The lid popped off, and books sprawled out from their upended container. He would have sworn, but he was too dejected to make that much effort. Had he been able to just slide down into the nearby storm drain and flow into dark oblivion, Alice was sure he would have chosen to do so just then. Just looking at him seemed to suck the energy from her mind and heart.

But just then Alice looked up to see a guy in his early twenties hustling across the street toward him. "Oh, I hope he's coming to help," she confided to her time-traveling companion and felt some relief as he reached down to help pick up the objects from the ground and replace them in the box.

"Now, Alice, concentrate very hard and reach out emotionally to feel the heart of this young man who came across the street to help. Unfortunately in today's world, many will only provide assistance to those who will benefit them. A true test of who someone is can be seen in how they act toward individuals and groups who can do absolutely nothing for them. It is easy to provide service or help someone if you know you will be helped in turn. However, those who have learned abundance will offer generously to others. As they give they receive, and as they receive they are more capable of giving."

"Guardian Angel, I feel so strongly within myself what motivated this person to help! He is focused 100% on this young man's troubled soul. It's as if he senses somehow that the kid's on his way to end his life. That poor kid is so full of despair that he needs an intervention with someone who will willingly give his all, and this other guy seems willing to do exactly that."

"Hey, man, don't bother. You don't need to help me with this stuff," the teenager murmured despondently.

"Are you kidding me? Nobody can carry all this alone. I'll help you, so where are we going?"

He replied without looking at his helper directly, "Well, home, but I can do it alone. Don't worry about me."

"Wouldn't hear of it. Lead the way, my friend. By the way, my name's Michael; what's yours?"

With her guardian angel's help, Alice could feel the heart of this kind young stranger. She listened as they talked about simple things as they walked, and could tell that the good Samaritan really cared about the dejected kid with the heavy load. He projected deep love and understanding that was slowly wearing away the dark cloud surrounding the younger man.

The guardian angel interrupted Alice's concentration to explain the situation in greater detail. "Alice, you need to know that this fellow who crossed the road to help has had a difficult life. Several years ago he attempted suicide and was rescued just before jumping to his death. He has since lived a life committed to others' needs and feelings, especially those who are especially despondent."

While en route to the younger man's home, the words spoken by the helpful stranger began to build his self-image, giving him a renewed sense of confidence, hope, and self-worth. No one but perhaps the guardian angel and now Alice could have seen the deep despair that this young man struggled against.

"Alice, this simple act of kindness altered the life path of a young man in need. He responded to someone who truly cared in the same way that the helpful stranger had responded to someone who helped him in a moment of intense need. Both of these young men went on to offer much to the world, but perhaps more important, they were constantly on the search for individuals needing a helping hand.

"When we feel down or alone, extending ourselves in the service of others helps to cure our ills too. Our inner feelings of discouragement or whatever may be getting us down are erased immediately by merely giving our all. As we give, loads are lightened, friendships built, lessons learned, skills enhanced, and love felt.

"In the world you live in, Alice, people are experiencing a time that leaves so many feeling hopeless. Such feelings are new to many, and they do not know how to handle them. People need the optimism of a brighter day. We need those who have served, like you and your family, to continue to serve, and we need to bring in those who have not yet offered their time and talents in improving the lives of those around us. We need a collective energy to enlighten, teach, and give hope.

"I make you a promise, my young student: as you give you will receive. Your life will be richly blessed and magnified tenfold. Test it, live it, and experience it. I promise you that as you alter and change for good the life of someone in need, your own life will change for the good as well. You feel the truth of my words in your heart—you have, you are, and you will make a difference to all you come in contact with, if you continue to commit totally to give of yourself.

"As you give you will receive; as you receive, you will be able to give more. Think of it as having a light within you. You can give light to others as long as it is burning inside you. It will never diminish or burn out from giving. In fact, you will learn that as the light is given, more light is generated, allowing for a brighter existence for all. And know this—if for some reason your light ever blows out, those you have ignited around you will be there to reignite your flame.

"And now for the most important lesson this evening: don't ever take away another's opportunity to serve. No one is always on the giving end of service. Life presents moments where being the recipient is just as necessary. For some this may be hard, seeming nearly impossible—-it isn't. Receive with the same joy you give, and your burdens will fade. Then, when you are back on top, you will be a better servant.

"Good night, Alice. Remember to record this in your journal. I will return soon to teach you again."

With that he was gone. Alice sensed the importance of writing before the clarity of the experience faded, so she sat at her desk and began writing:

When we serve, we experience; when we experience, we teach; when we teach, we learn; when we learn, our lives are permanently changed; and as our lives are changed, we are enriched beyond our wildest dreams.

I give of myself willingly; as I do, I receive which allows me to give more.

I am honest and generous.

Nature, by example, shows us that our personal development comes over time. Anything worthwhile grows methodically, building on a strong foundation. Develop a willingness to carry on despite roadblocks.

Chapter 23

Alice was exhausted as she turned back the covers and prepared for bed. Today had been incredibly long. Remembering the value of giving service that she had learned from the angel, last week she had volunteered to help at the community center one night a week, helping learning-challenged children.

It had seemed like such a good idea at the time, but she had never taken on this particular challenge before. A fourth-grade boy named Jake was having problems with subtraction, and it seemed to Alice that she had explained how to subtract 5 oranges from 8 oranges right around 250 times. And she was not sure that Jake would remember a single thing she had said by tomorrow morning.

"Hello, Alice. Rough day?"

"Something like that."

"I've got something to visit with you, if you think you could deal with me for a few minutes."

"Of course! I hope I'm never too tired for you, old friend."

"You've probably heard the statement that patience is a virtue sometime in your life, haven't you, Alice?"

"Yes, earlier this evening, as a matter of fact!" she laughed. "Of course, you probably knew that, didn't you!"

"I might have had a clue about your day, I admit. But seriously, today more than ever we need to understand the value of patience. The world today is experiencing an increasing need for instant gratification. Technology is a big part, offering quicker and quicker response times. Go back just a few years and see what was acceptable then. Today, meeting those same timelines is deemed inadequate, and it is getting worse!

"Nature offers the best example. When we plant a new crop, we must be patient. New plants don't grow overnight. To be strong plants need rich soil, water, sunlight, removal of weeds, and added nutrients.

"Often in life, when we want things now, when we can't wait, nothing works to our favor. Nature doesn't allow haste; anything worthwhile takes time and proper attention to detail. For us to be strong, our growth must come over time.

"I am aware of a study that was done in which scientists tested children's ability to delay instant gratification in order to receive a promised greater reward. In this study, the children sat at a table with a single marshmallow. They could eat the treat immediately if they desired or wait for fifteen minutes and be given more. The children were then left alone with this simple decision placed before them, while the scientists observed from a different room.

"Some immediately picked up the marshmallow and began eating it, then sat waiting for someone to reenter the room. Others sat fidgeting, moving restlessly and clearly debating with themselves. Often this second group of children refrained from eating the treat for an average of half the fifteen-minute time frame. After waiting a fair amount of time, many then reached out, grabbed their marshmallow, and began eating the treat. They would take bites, eating the treat slower than the first group. The last group, clearly having made up their mind from the beginning, sat patiently waiting for the fifteen minutes to pass. They knew time would pass quickly, and then they would enjoy their reward. This last group, which demonstrated such patience, represented nearly thirty percent of the entire group.

"This study didn't prove anything other than to suggest that some kids will wait while others don't, perhaps expecting instant gratification. Some will settle for having less now, while others clearly see the advantage in a short demonstration of endurance.

"But the study didn't end there. Those who had waited for the greater reward also achieved more later in life. The group who waited had more college degrees, higher paying jobs, and higher net worth than nearly all those in the other groups. These extended findings provided greater insight than the original findings, which only suggested something about immediate gratification.

"Can we gain greater understanding of why an exercise of patience provides access to a better life?"

The old monk extended his hand to Alice, who now understood the gesture to mean that they were going to have an incredible experience together. Holding hands, Alice and her guardian angel entered a room where a woman was just preparing to go to bed. She sat on the bed and wept with her face buried deep in her hands. As she did so, Alice could hear her murmur: "How on earth will I survive another day?"

Now accustomed to feeling the emotions of the people that the two of them visited in this fasion, Alice could sense that this woman felt the weight of her entire known world on her—any more pressure would bring a complete collapse.

Part of the problem was that her boss was an emotional sponge: continuously throughout the day he would come to her for validation that all was going to be okay. Going to work meant her last ounce of sanity was instantly stripped by having to carry her unstable leader's emotional burdens.

But that was not all. She had three children: Candace, 15; Brent, 12; and Mindy, 10. Now that they were out of school for the summer, they demanded attention. Time had been easier to give when money wasn't such a high priority. The family had been hit hard by the failing economy, and employment that had once been enjoyment had now became a fundamental need, a burden just to keep food on the table.

It seemed to this woman as though little things that used to be incidental now were magnified to gigantic proportions. Slowly she slid from the edge of the bed to the floor, where she knelt in prayer. The knowledge she carried in her heart was that her Creator wouldn't test her beyond her ability to sustain, yet she was in mental and physical pain. She didn't know how much further she could go.

"Guardian Angel, I feel the weight of her burdens so powerfully that I can scarcely breathe. Her emotional pain is nearly suffocating. How can I learn anything positive from such a crushing situation?"

But he offered no response other than to incline his head in her direction, indicating that she should continue engaging in the experience of watching and feeling.

Somehow quieting her sobs for a moment, the woman took a deep breath and began to pray. She pled for relief, suggesting that the energy she asked for would be put to good use. She wanted only to be a good mother and employee. She recognized that her previously clear appreciation for all she possessed now was clouded by an unending concentration on difficulties. The last words she offered struck Alice with remarkable power: "Please, God, if there is no relief, give me understanding."

At last the monk spoke: "Alice, what this mother doesn't understand is that she is almost there. Now feel, Alice, what she learns in her heart. Search in your soul and feel deeply what the answer to her prayer is."

Alice felt a cleansing wave of calmness wash over her as she realized this mother's answer—she had nearly completed her voyage. All she needed was a little more patience and all would be well.

"Patience is the secret to a life of happiness. You might think of it as staying power, endurance, persistence, or even tolerance, but mostly it is realizing that when we are faced with difficult situations, we must set aside any self-imposed time lines and have the maturity to take the time for the seed of experience to fully mature. Remember what we learned from nature.

"When you think, Alice, of what you treasure in life, you will realize that the most precious gifts come through patience. As you recognize the traits of those who are successful in life, you will see at the heart of their character extraordinary patience."

Alice slept well that night, but before she did she took time to write in her journal:

I do not need instant gratification. Time builds a strong foundation for growth. I will put in the time for valued outcomes.

I am honest, generous, and patient.

Purity in thought and deed build lasting relationships; with valued loved ones, nothing can destroy us.

Chapter 24

Alice loved Saturday mornings for a variety of reasons. Usually she loved to catch up on her sleep, snuggled deep under the soft flannel sheets she had learned to appreciate on a family vacation to British Columbia two years ago. Sometimes she loved to toss those sheets aside and spend the morning just visiting with her mother in the kitchen over a bowl of Lucky Charms. But today she loved Saturday mornings for the peace she could find on the well-groomed trails of a nature park not far from her home. Though her parents warned her against walking there alone late at night, Saturday mornings brought just enough foot traffic in the park to be safe but enough solitude to be able to think well.

This morning she was feeling particularly contemplative, and her pace reflected it, valuing her new inner peace, understanding, and patience so well learned in her last lesson. She chose a leisurely gait on an easy trail that meandered back and forth across a beautiful little stream. Some mornings would have found her attacking a more aggressive trail up the hillside, but this morning she preferred mental exertion to physical.

The morning light danced on the trail as the sun peeked and poked its way through the quaking aspens that surrounded this whole area. Maybe that's why she loved to walk here. She had heard once in a biology class that large groves of aspens are all connected at the root level, sometimes forming acres and acres of a single organic structure. That underlying connectedness somehow always helped her find harmony within herself.

When Alice had been an eighth-grader, she had met Monique, a delightful foreign exchange student from France. They had several classes together each day, and they had formed a close friendship for the five months that Monique had been a fellow student. Since then, they usually kept track of each other via Facebook, writing to each other at least every week or so. But Alice had not heard from Monique for nearly a week and a half, and on Thursday she had been shocked to see that her little friend had changed her status to "Pregnant and not a bit happy about it."

So here she was, walking her favorite trail and looking for understanding, solace, and some sort of direction on what she should do. She was beginning to feel the peace of the park when she neared the loop in the trail that meant it was time to cross the creek and head back down the other side toward the trail head. Standing in the center of the footbridge built of redwood planks and staring very intently at the morning light playing with the water as it bounced about the rocks that lined the bottom of the stream was a very familiar figure.

Alice walked up alongside her Cambodian guardian angel and asked, "So, stranger, what brings you to these parts? Don't tell me that angels need to go hiking for their health!"

Smiling, the wizened man replied, "No, Alice, not for our physical health anyway. But everyone needs a little refresher spiritually from time to time. This is a very good place, but then, I believe you already know that. Can you hear the trees?"

"Do they talk to you?"

"Better than that, they hum! Hold my hand for a moment, little one."

Alice placed her hands around his right hand comfortably and closed her eyes. Slowly she became aware of what she had to agree was a soft hum, as if the aspens were practicing their communal yoga and were all voicing the universal "Om" sound of eastern mystics. Whatever it was, it was healing and wholesome, if sounds can be described in that way.

She opened her eyes, and the angel gently withdrew his hand from hers. "Thank you, old friend. That was amazing! Are we we going to do the time travel thing this morning? That was so rad that I still almost can't believe it!"

"No, Alice, not today. Today I want to just chat with you here by this pure stream in this wonderful aspen grove about a very, very important principle.

"Alice, have you ever heard your parents or grandparents say, 'How will our children make it through these times?' Or 'How will our family ever survive what is happening to our world?'

"These feelings usually come from those who are older, perhaps thinking they would not survive what your generation faces today. Drugs are easily obtained, pornography is rampant—"

"Yeah," Alice interrupted, "and technology has created an avenue of instant gratification for so many things, as you have taught me."

"Good, Alice, I am impressed. I've told you before just how special you are. I am not sure I could have been as strong as you are today. It seems to me that things were not as tough for my generation as what your generation is faced with. I believe you and your peers across the world are the strongest generation to live on this earth.

"In some ways, this morning perhaps will be the most difficult topic I will share with you, Alice. I know of your concern for your friend Monique. But this issue lies much closer at home than you might think. Your sister Lucy was recently presented with a circumstance where she was mocked for being chaste. Her friends who found she is not engaged in adult activities made fun of her commitment.

"Lucy has self-elected to wait until marriage to participate in what she sees as behavior typically reserved for married adults. Her friends couldn't understand that and told her that she will never have fun or know if she is compatible physically with her partner. One of them told her, 'If you wait, you might find out too late that you just are just not meant to be life partners. What will you do then? Sex is one of the most important things you will do when you do get married—you're stupid if you don't find out whether you're going to get along in the bedroom as well as in the kitchen!'"

"I know that my parents and my faith have very consistently taught that we should wait until marriage for marital intimacy, but that girl does sort of have a point. I mean, couldn't that prevent a lot of divorces? But then you run the risk of being 'pregnant and not liking it a bit.' What's the answer? Please teach me so that I can learn and strengthen my friends."

"You know, Alice, there are some real advantages in being an angel. One of them is that we get to change our minds. Please take my hand—I think I will show you something after all."

"Oh, gladly!" Off the two went to the time and place where Alice's sister was engaged in a conversation with her friends.

"Wow, Lucy is really upset! I can feel that she wants desperately to be able to share her feelings with her friends but is frustrated that she can't get through."

"You are right, Alice; however, I want you to feel what Lucy's friends are feeling right now. Okay? Start with the young lady over there who is not talking at all."

Alice could feel the heart of the young lady—she felt deeply the truth of what Lucy was saying, but wondered to herself whether she could ever be so strong as to fight through the peer pressures. After all, that had been the only reason she had participated up until now.

"Guardian Angel, that is sad to me. Lucy doesn't feel anyone is listening, yet this girl believes with all her heart. She is only unaware of how to gain the strength so obvious in Lucy."

"Exactly. Now go over to the girl who just called your sister a prude and made fun of her."

"Oh, my gosh, no way! She totally believes what Lucy is saying in her heart but can't find a way out of her current situation. She thinks that her boyfriend won't like her if she stops having sex with him. All she is hoping for is a way to get to the place Lucy is describing without losing what she feels she has."

"Yes, mostly that is true. But she also wonders if there is anything to her relationship beyond the physical attractions.

"Alice, the attraction and drive we all have and enjoy are natural and necessary. These feelings are some of the most intimate you will ever experience in life—if done in the proper time and place.

"These young kids are caught in satisfying base emotions that leave no lasting or meaningful relationship. The young ladies go home brokenhearted, knowing that giving up intimacy wasn't worth it. They have fallen into a trap which gets deeper and deeper over time.

"Relationships such as these in later life lead to fear of infidelity or resentment of wandering eyes. If the gift of building unity come after these kids find commonality, love, excitement, and enjoyment of being together, the experience becomes magnified.

"Being together only for the satisfaction of a moment of physical pleasure creates no internal joy or long-term satisfaction.

"Now hold my hand one more time please."

∞ ∞ ∞

Suddenly they were standing on the edge of a rundown refugee camp in Cambodia. "Angel, this looks familiar. Have I been here before?"

"Very good, Alice. Yes, you have been here. But I don't think you were aware of something that your brother, Rick, experienced during the few hours that you were here. Watch and see what he learned."

Rick Callister got the best of his parents' genes—his father's powerful swimmer's build and naturally big heart combined with his mother's sensitivity and propensity to serve the less fortunate. Like his parents, he seemed to attract people wherever he went and often found himself at the center of whatever group of individuals was on hand. But unlike them, he was by nature shy and reserved. This combination of inherent shyness and irresistible charm sometimes made for an interesting situation.

When the Callisters arrived at the first refugee camp that they visited in Cambodia, they were already several-day veterans of providing service to people whom they could not communicate well with. They relied on local authorities and more specifically on Tree to ensure that communications took place as they should, and for the most part this proved to be a very successful arrangement. Now and then, however, the cultural barrier caused unintentional problems.

So it was for Rick in the small refugee village of Svay Rieng. Shortly after they arrived, Rick and his father were handing out mosquito nets when Rick's eyes were drawn to a teenage girl of approximately his age standing on the edge of those who awaited nets. She was slight of build, had jet-black straight hair, and a certain air of mystery about her that Rick found irresistible. And then she was gone.

Thirty minutes later she reappeared. The crowd was smaller, the wait shorter. As she slowly through attrition made her way to the front of the line, Rick could see the reason for her absence, or so he supposed. At her feet were two large metal pails of water, which she shuffled along in front of her as she moved along.

How she had carried them was beyond Rick's comprehension, for his many years of swimming had taught him to appreciate the weight of even a small amount of water.

At last it was her turn, and she looked hopefully up and Jim and then Rick. Jim was taken aback at the sincere beauty of her eyes and the honesty of her gaze. For Rick, the experience was multipled several fold. Speechless, he simply stared back. He could do nothing else. "How many in your family?" Jim asked quietly. Reverence somehow seemed the most natural emotion for the task at hand.

She held up the fingers of one hand and responded in hesitant but practiced English, "Four, sir." Normally at this point, Rick would pull the requested number of nets from the truck and hand them to his father, who would in turn hand them over to the requesting individual. Always a smile of thanks and a polite bow was offered in return as a show of respect and gratitude. But Rick was frozen to his view of this most beautiful sight in his life, and he just didn't know what to do. Typically his shyness drove him to simply head off to a quiet corner where he could spend a minute or two until someone would spot him and be drawn to come speak to him. Today, duty required him to stay in his place while attraction made him want to hide. He was stuck in between, and every neuron in his system seemed to be calling a conflicting direction to his brain.

"Son? Four nets for the young lady?"

"Oh, yeah . . . sure, Dad. I'll, uh, I'll get them." And so he did. And then as he started to hand them to his father, his brain finally began to function. How is this slight young lady going to carry two pails of water, plus these four nets? He would simply have to help. And so Rick found himself pulling the nets back from his dad's outstretched hands and speaking, aloud. "Uh, Dad, maybe I'd better help her get these home. I mean, she's got this water to deal with, and now four packages of mosquito netting, and she's not exactly built like a football player."

Jim smiled. He'd been watching the young lady out of the corner of his eye, and although she was being quite discreet, something told him that there was a reason why she had waited until nearly the end and had increased her burden by fetching the water before coming after the nets. *Seems like women make the world go round regardless of what country you're in,* he thought to himself, and then responded as innocently as he could muster, "Rick, I think that would be a great idea! There are only a handful of people left here to take care of, and I think I can handle them on my own just fine."

With that, Rick stepped past his father and approached the girl in front of him. "Hello, my name is Rick. Do you speak English?"

Deliberately, as one would expect to hear in a school recitation, she responded, "Hello, Rick. My name is Chetnah. I speak English some, but you must speak slow, yes?"

"Chetnah—that is a beautiful name. May I help you carry your things to your home? Perhaps I could carry the water pails, if you could manage these nets. I think that the water will be much heavier than these nets."

"Thank you. Please, give nets to me. I show you way to my house."

Rick picked up the pails, looked at his father as if to say, "I'll find you later!" and turned to follow his new friend. Along the way, they exchanged pleasantries and learned of each other's families and general likes and dislikes. Rick was a swirling mix of intrigue, shyness, boldness in a new adventure, and natural interest in someone very different than he had ever met before. Little did he know that his new friend was feeling nearly the exact same range of emotions.

The camp was not so large that it took very long to arrive at their destination, but it was long enough for the two young people from different sides of the world to learn that there was an unmistakable attraction between them. It didn't make any kind of sense—they spoke different languages, had completely different cultural backgrounds, believed in different Gods, dealt with very different living circumstances, and yet there they were—feeling their way through an uncertain territory that neither understood and both very much wanted to explore.

As they walked, small clouds of dust rose with each footfall on the arid ground between the makeshift huts of the refugee village. Each hut was a little different than the rest, although the materials were pretty much common among them. The basic outline of each structure was made of poles lashed together. Walls consisted of corrugated steel, handwoven mats of reeds and palm leaves, and anything else that could be leaned against or tied to the pole outlines. Most roofs were made of tarps draped over the top of the hut, although that too could be augmented by corrugated steel or handwoven mats. The floor was raised off the dirt by twelve to eighteen inches, presumably to make it more difficult for rodents and small animals to gain access to the floor surface, which was also where the people slept. They would roll out a small sleeping mat on the floor made of sticks and poles lashed together and sleep right there on the floor.

One of the dangers of such an arrangement was that the sleepers were constantly victimized by mosquitoes during the night, mosquitoes that brought with them deadly malaria. The hot nights prevented the use of even the lightest bed sheets, had such things existed, and the makeshift homes were so open that insects could have free run of the place. That was why the mosquito nets that the Callister family had brought to the village were so important. The nets were proven life savers, particularly to the young and aged of the population. Chetnah and her fellow refugees were so excited to receive the nets that they viewed the family from America as true heroes. But this handsome young man, he had an extra dose of specialness about him!

So within a matter of a few minutes, Chetnah and Rick arrived at their destination. Chetnah handled the introductions to her parents and her younger brother, and then the two teenagers worked together to quickly demonstrate the nets to her family and then set them up so they would be out of the way during the day and easily and effectively positioned for sleeping at night.

And then it was suddenly awkward. Had they been at Rick's home in the United States, he probably would have asked Chetnah if she would like to watch television or play a game on their Wii in the family room, stopping to grab a couple of sodas from the refrigerator on the way. But this was not his home, and her home had neither television, Wii, family room, or refrigerator. In fact, it had only one room, and that room was also occupied by her entire family. Awkward.

"So, Chetnah, how about showing me around a little? Would that be okay?"

She looked to her parents and translated. Rick saw the hint of a smile on her mother's face, while her father's eyebrows raised slightly but otherwise showed no emotion. He did, however, nod ever so slightly to indicate that she could do as she proposed and go for a brief walk with this American boy. He seemed nice enough, but he was American, after all, and Americans sometimes had the reputation of being self-centered womanizers. The father's rare experiences with Americans had not disproven that idea.

"Come with me, Rick. I show you our little camp." Rick smiled nervously and nodded a grateful good-bye to Chetnah's parents, then followed her out through the opening that served as a doorway and on to path that also served as a road to connect all the "houses" on that "street."

Tree, the Callisters' faithful driver and translator, had just delivered a message to one of the overseers of the refugee camp and was on his way back to the family when he saw Rick and Chetnah leaving her shack. The attraction between them was obvious, so Tree watched from a distance as they began to walk about the exterior of the camp. Stopping under the shade of a tree, they playfully exchanged a light banter that Tree could not quite hear. But the occasional light touch of a hand on a shoulder or arm was unmistakable, and Tree became concerned about the messages being sent between the two because they lacked the cultural background of the other required to read those messages properly. When the youngsters left the tree to continue their walk, Tree left in search of Karen Callister. She would know whether his concerns were valid or not.

"Oh, hello, Tree. Were you able to deliver my message to the Schwimmers? Where would they like us to leave the few mosquito nets that were not distributed? I'm sure they will be able to put them to good use as more people move into the camp here."

"Yes, Mrs. Callister, she was most grateful that you would leave them for her. She said that we should not just leave them lying unattended; if you could keep them with you for just a few more minutes, she will be along shortly to retrieve them."

"Thank you, Tree. That was kind of you to track her down for us. Did you happen to see that son of mine anywhere as you were walking across the camp?"

"Again I must say yes, Mrs. Callister. May I be so bold as to ask for a minute of your time, please?"

"Tree, but of course. What can I do for you? Does it have anything to do with Rick? Is he okay? Jim told me he went to help deliver some nets and carry water for a young woman who needed some help."

"He is quite okay. I think that they both enjoyed fulfilling that task, if you know what I mean. Rick is a very handsome young man with a smile that would turn the head of any girl in the world. And Chetnah, the girl he is helping, is quite attractive herself. I believe they have been smitten by the other. In fact, I just saw them walking on the far side of the camp, and they seemed to be having a wonderful time."

"Oh, Tree, this might sound odd for me to say, but that might be just what Rick needs. I agree that he is what we in the United States would call a 'babe magnet.' But he doesn't realize it; in fact, he is quite shy and has little confidence around girls. Something like this might be very good for his self-image."

"That might be true, Mrs. Callister. But he must also be careful. Gestures or actions that might mean one thing to you as an American might mean something very different in our culture. For example, French men kiss each other lightly on the cheek as a form of greeting, but in the United States that formal action will make many men very, very uncomfortable. You might get punched if you tried that to a cowboy, from what I have read.

"In a similar way, when a young man kisses a young woman in Cambodia, he has just indicated that he has selected that young woman for marriage. A kiss in this way is a promise to create a lifetime bond, even if they are separated for a time. This became very confusing to many of our young girls during what you know as the Vietnam War, because American servicemen would befriend them and kiss them as part of the American dating process, but to our girls those kisses were equivalent to a proposal of marriage.

"I do not say that Rick will try to kiss this girl, but they have found that they have an immediate fondness for each other. If he out of innocence expresses that fondness with a brief hug and simple kiss, and then returns home to the United States, she will never marry another, for in her mind she is betrothed to Rick Callister. Now, I do not wish to offend you, Mrs. Callister, but you know your son better than anyone in this half of the world, I believe. If this is information that he needs to have, would you do him—and his new friend—the honor of sharing it with him, for their mutual happiness. In Cambodia, we become friends first, and then we love. After learning to love well and appropriately, we then consider becoming lovers. I see the Schwimmers headed our way. May I take care of the nets with them? I see a young couple headed our way whom you might like to visit with."

Sure enough, Karen looked to the east to see the familiar amble of her only son, accompanied by the soft glide of Chetnah, the girl at his side. Immediately she perceived with her mother's instincts that Tree had spoken truly, for as they walked, they looked for opportunities to touch in some way—flicking a fly from a shoulder, a touch on the arm to draw attention, or any of a dozen ways to signal someone that you like them and want to make sure that they don't miss the clue. Though Rick was shy, she knew that some motherly advice was appropriate—and soon.

"Hello, Rick!" she called. "I see you have found a tour guide to get you out of work."

"I didn't know—I mean, I thought we—Dad said I could—" he stammered.

"I'm just kidding, son!" she laughed warmly. "We've done all that we came to do. Now we're all just enjoying a little time to relax and get to know the people here. And that," she said as she turned towards his companion for the afternoon, "seems to be exactly what you're doing. So, introduce me to your friend, will you?"

"Geez, Mom. Don't play me like that, although you did get me good! This is Chetnah, the foremost expert on the sights and sounds of Svay Rieng. She's been showing me around, and doing an excellent job of it, I must say. And Chetnah, this lovely young lady might look like my sister, but she is really my mother." Karen extended her hand for a friendly handshake, and Chetnah responded warmly.

"I am not sure I am best tour guide, but Rick is good student. You have nice son, Mrs. Callister."

"Thank you, Chetnah. He is a good son with many talents, which I won't mention now for fear of embarrassing him. I'm sorry to interrupt your tour for a just a minute, but could I speak with your student for three minutes about some family matters? Please just stay right here, and I'll return him to you quickly." Rick looked at his mother quizzically, but her body language gave him no clues as to what she had in mind.

"Of course, Mrs. Callister. Please take your time, and I will wait in the shade over there."

"Oh, please call me Karen. I promise I'll return him to you very shortly—right to the pavilion." Karen hooked her arm through her son's and walked off a few paces, talking quietly as she did. "Rick, she's cute! You two seem to have really hit it off very quickly, huh?"

"Oh, Mom, it's not like love at first sight. She's just different, and there's something that is very familiar about her. But I promise I'm not going to try to sneak her into my carry-on bag when we leave here." He smiled slyly and continued, "Although, I can't make the same promise about my big bag. I have a lot of space in there now that we've given away all those quilts that Grandma and her friends made."

Karen laughed. She did love this boy of hers. "Well, Rick, that's actually what I wanted to talk to you about. I don't want to squash a new friendship, but I do need to share some things about Cambodian culture that you should be aware of." Without lecturing, Karen then quickly shared with Rick what she had just learned from Tree. "Now, Rick, I'm not trying to embarrass you or change anything about what you and Chetnah are doing here. I just want to make sure that you send the signals that you really want to send without unintentionally hurting someone who is important to you. Now, I think I've kept you quite long enough. You'd best get over to the pavilion before she finds someone else to give tours to, okay?"

"Hey, Mom, thanks for how you handled that. For an older woman, you're not so bad!" And off he trotted, a small puff of dust rising from each foot fall.

∞ ∞ ∞

"And that, Alice, was how Rick and Chetnah met for the first time. I think they will always have a special friendship that none of us expected nor can we explain. It's a story I will never forget. What have you learned?"

"I didn't realize just how deeply Cambodians felt about simple things like holding hands and kissing. I guess some cultures must seem pretty loose to them. To be honest, if I had to choose which I would prefer, I think that knowing the boundaries of right and wrong as your people do makes me feel cleaner personally and just better about life in general."

"Alice, your peers are bright, have limited fear, challenge thought, overcome difficulty, and are full of compassion. They are truly incredible! I can't wait to see the inventions they develop, the frontiers they explore, and the ills they extinguish permanently.

"I pray they will discover the value of living by the guidance of their hearts and reserve base desires for the times when they will bring true happiness. This will assist them in their growth, and together we will rejoice in their ability."

Later when Alice got home from her morning hike, she opened her journal and wrote:

Love can be disguised as a physical desire. I will build my relationships first, knowing there are special times ahead.

I am honest, generous, patient, and virtuous.

Show empathy and charity to all—seeing others from their perspective opens our minds. Observe, knowing that it is more important what others sense than how we feel.

Chapter 25

"Hey, dude, chill out will you! You're such a ride psycho!"

"No kidding, man! The monkey cage is on the other side of the park. Is this the first time your keeper has let you outside?"

"And this, children, is why you should never do drugs!"

Alice looked away from the three young teenage boys and toward her cousin Eric, then giggled. How could you not enjoy the pure excitement that exuded from the screams that just flowed unbidden from inside as they stood in line, waiting for the roller coaster! And had Eric been four or five years old, no one else in line would have thought anything of his antics either. But Eric was three years her senior and autistic. Tall, slender, with disarming dimples and active blue eyes, had Eric not been blessed with autism he might well have been viewed as any other successful college student home for a weekend break. But Eric was Eric, and the comments coming from these seventh-grade boys were beginning to get on her nerves. She had learned to ignore innocent comments that people made out of ignorance, but these boys were becoming just cruel. It was time to rein them in a bit.

"Eric, wait right here for me, will you?" And turning to the person behind them in line, she said, "I'll be right back," and she walked towards the troublemakers. "Hey, guys, what's up?"

Alice had a gift. Blonde, blue-eyed, nicely tanned, and athletic, she was a people magnet. And when she wanted to be, she was especially a boy magnet. She was an accomplished gymnast and knew how to walk and move with just enough mystery to turn the head of any healthy young man. For this attractive young lady to even acknowledge the presence of those three boys was enough to make all three of them stumble over each other in a rush to please her.

"Hey, babe! What can we do for you?" the largest of the

three said with mock bravado. It was all Alice could do to not burst out in laughter. This wasn't the first time that she had encountered a young man who was out of his league in trying to impress her. "We need a fourth to make up our car on the coaster. Wanna join us?"

"As tempting as that sounds, I've already got a date. Sorry, boys," she nearly purred.

Startled, the three looked around, expecting the worst. "Relax, guys. He's right here. Hey, Eric, come here and meet my new friends."

Eric grinned at her and hopped like a frog over to his cousin. Alice warmly slid her arm around him and squeezed. "Guys, this is Eric. This is my favorite day of the year, because every year on this day, Eric and I come to this amusement park and have the most amazing time." Her eyes twinkled as she leaned over and gave him a little kiss on the cheek. "I tell people that he's my boyfriend because he's so darn handsome, but he's really my cousin. Isn't that right, Eric?"

Eric grinned, "Alice is my best cousin girlfriend ever! Let's go ride, Alice."

"We will, Eric. I just wanted you to meet these handsome young men." Turning away from Eric to face the three youngsters directly, she spoke openly, "Eric is autistic. Today he is the most important person in my life. Let me tell you a secret about older girls. Nothing impresses a girl as much as a guy who is willing to make sure that kids like Eric have a good time at an amusement park. A man who can do that, well, he's just hot!"

The ringleader gave Eric a high five, winked at Alice, and said, "Eric, you're a stud! Don't lose your place in line—it's almost your turn. And Alice, you've got a cool date. But our offer stands—you can ride with us anytime that your 'boyfriend' needs a break."

"Thanks, guys. I'll remember that." Alice and Eric slid back into their places in line, and five minutes later were climbing into a roller coaster car. Eric screamed and laughed the whole ride, and when their car pulled in to unload and get a new set of passengers, Eric found that he had a cheering section waiting for him—led by three junior high boys who wanted to make sure he was having a good time, just in case any good-looking girls were watching.

That evening, Alice took Eric home—tired, in fact she had to wake him when she pulled into his driveway, but very, very happy. And so was Alice. She had been completely honest earlier in the day at describing this annual outing as her "favorite day of the year."

As she sat down later at home to make some notes in her diary about the day, she tried something a little different. Usually she waited for her guardian angel to contact her, but she was so excited about the day with Eric that she wanted to share with her old friend. Calling out to the space in her bedroom in a general way, she began, "Hey, Guardian Angel! I'm not really sure if the rules allow me to request a visit, but this seemed like a good time to try. So how about it—any words of wisdom for me today?"

Suddenly, as if fading into existence, over next to the window, Alice thought she saw a glimmer. As she focused, an outline became visible, then the full shape, and finally all the details of her now-familiar guide. "When I saw how you were spending the day, I thought I should reserve the evening for a little chat. Looks like you had the same thing in mind!"

"Oh, what a fantastic day I had today. Eric is such a special kid, and I love him so much!"

"But not everyone felt the same about him wherever you went in the park."

"True, but that's only because not every knows him."

"That is precisely what I'd like to talk about this evening. Alice, do you remember the day you and your father encountered the bikers last spring in Phoenix?"

"Sure. We went for a walk just to get out of the hotel for a while; it was in a good neighborhood, and we felt quite safe, but we turned a corner while walking and found ourselves walking past a whole row of Harleys parked on the side of the road, with the riders standing together in a group. I was pretty nervous, but my dad, well, you know how he is, he loves Harleys and he loves people, so he stopped to admire the bikes.

"I guess there were a couple of bikes that were pretty rare, and my dad recognized them for what they were. Before long, he and the bikers were talking about 'hogs' as if they were best friends. When we first saw these tough-looking bikers, I was sure they were going to kill us. But my dad saw past all the leather and tattoos and treated them like regular people. Before we left, they let my dad take me for a ride on a couple of the bikes, with an open invitation to stop any time we were in town and hang out with them."

"Alice, too many people in this world make assumptions about others based on stereotypes or other unfair criteria. Remember how you felt when those boys today were making fun of Eric? They were judging him unfairly. But you did the same thing when you thought that all bikers are convicts and drug runners. Did you know that biker groups are some of the best grass roots fundraisers for children in the country?"

"You never cease to impress me! How did a girl like me ever get so lucky to have the best guardian angel who ever lived?"

"Alice, there is no luck involved in the assignment of guardian angels. You have been watched for your entire life. As I was saying a minute ago, it is important to watch, observe things for what they truly are, feel closely with your heart to see what others' true intentions are, and then act accordingly. With practice, you will learn to discern people more quickly. For now, never forget the lessons learned with Eric, the bikers, and the evil men in Angkor Wat. There is something to be learned from each experience.

"Sleep well, and sleep safely this evening, little one. Ninja Monk is watching." He chuckled gently at his own joke, and walked over to the window. Alice watched as his image blurred, dimmed, and disappeared. Had she not known better, she might have wondered whether he had been there at all. But she did know, and that made all the difference.

Turning back to her journal she wrote:

We must see others from the inside. I observe closely, feel clearly, and choose wisely how I perceive all those I am blessed to meet.

I am honest, generous, patient, virtuous, and kind.

Maintain composure in times of heightened emotion, reacting only when thoughts are calm and clear. Being sensible will open doors for solutions and creativity.

Chapter 26

Alice was intrigued, to say the least. This morning when she got up, she found an envelope—sitting on the bathroom counter right between her ceramic hair straightener and her favorite hairbrush. But this was not just any old white security envelope containing your basic Hallmark card, as sweet and wonderful as Hallmark cards can be. No, this was an invitation, the envelope addressed simply to "Alice," but written in beautiful handpainted lettering in black ink, using a fine horsehair brush. The envelope was custom-made, if not hand-made, from a fine linen paper, with purposefully adorned rough edging.

Inside the envelope was a single sheet of paper of the same hand-made but exquisite quality as the envelope. On the paper, in a beautiful flowing hand, was this note:

Little One,

Today is the fifth anniversary of our first meeting. To celebrate, I have arranged to take you to a movie this afternoon (angels don't carry a lot of cash, so I hope you don't mind the matinee!). I will meet you at 5:15 in front of the ice cream shop by the mall's movie theater.

GA

Well, this should prove to be an interesting date, thought Alice. Aside from the fact that he is no longer among the living and he is a dedicated monk, it's just a routine date with a friend. Yeah, right! Well, whatever he has up his sleeve, I'm sure I'll end up learning something.

At noon, she received a text from her father: "Picking up your mother for an early dinner date. Johanna is going to the high school football game. You're on your own for finding something to eat. Text us if you go anywhere." And so she did. She went home after school, made her favorite peanut butter and honey on wheat sandwich, got her homework out of the way, and then caught the bus over to the mall, sending her parents a text before she left that she was "going to a movie with a friend but won't be late."

As promised, sitting at a small table in front of the ice cream shop by the theater sat a monk. He was sipping on a straw, the bottom end of which was in a medium-sized Dr. Pepper, and when he saw Alice approaching his eyes lit up, indeed his whole face lit up.

"Alice! I'm so delighted that you came!"

"How could I possibly turn down such an offer—a movie date with such a handsome angel?"

"Ah, my little Alice. You have become so precious to me. We have learned a lot together, haven't we? It has been wonderful for me to teach you.

"Today we will learn one of life's greatest lessons—to master emotion in times of intense feelings. Words are described as being stronger than a sword. At times when we react negatively because we feel strongly and say something that might actually be inappropriate, and then later realize that what was spoken cannot be retrieved, we sense how devastating our words were. Oh, if only we had maintained our composure or at least had insight to count to ten before reacting!

"You can see how quickly communication falls apart or how quickly it is restored by remaining even keeled. Now it's time for us to participate in a simple experience together in the movie theater."

"Now, this is a new twist—we are going somewhere you haven't been to see something that hasn't happened yet?"

"Alice, you are bright beyond your years. We will get into this at another time."

"Well, my guardian angel, I will not let you off this one. You definitely owe me an explanation about how this future viewing stuff works."

"Right now, it's time for us to go to a show—one that just happens to take place during a movie. I've already purchased the tickets, so let's go find a good place to sit." The old monk produced two tickets from a pocket somewhere in his robes, and together they walked to the theater. Inside, the lights were still on as the standard advertisers were still showing their spots. The theater was slowly filling, but there was still a pocket of seats open about halfway up the theater's stadium steps on the left-hand side. Alice followed her "date," who chose two seats right on the end of a row at the top of the open seats. Secretly she wondered what it took for an angel to arrange the seating in just the right way for whatever he had planned, but that was also a topic for another time.

Seconds after they had settled into their seats, two more people came into the theater—a young girl and her father. They sat one row ahead of the Alice and the angel and about two seats to their right. As they began to talk, it became clear that their family had come on hard times.

The young girl seemed mature beyond her years. She consoled her father that all would be okay and that she loved him. As they spoke, Alice felt an unbidden tear trickle down her cheek, thinking how fortunate this father was to have the love and support of his daughter. The young girl had just commented on how long it had been since her father had taken the time to relax. She reminded her dad of past times when they had gone to movies together, sitting, talking, crying, and laughing. These were times she missed, as she knew her dad did as well, but he had dedicated himself fully to correcting the ills the economy had placed on their family's finances.

It became obvious that they had chosen the matinee because the tickets were less expensive. They had bought a small value drink and popcorn and were sharing it happily. Alice gleaned from their quiet conversation that this young lady had saved her money from tending to have enough to allow them to enjoy this daddy-daughter date, as they used to go on. The father expressed gratitude for this expression of love, promising the girl they would get back to the good old times soon.

Next, entering while talking on a cell phone, was a woman who appeared to be rushed and impatient. Her cell phone was propped between her right shoulder and her cheek, in her left hand she held a large popcorn, and in her right she carried a large drink and an oversized purse. She took a seat two rows down from and directly in front of Alice, continuing to talk angrily on the cell phone all the while. Alice tried to be understanding, but the woman really was behaving quite obnoxiously.

Somehow she managed to slide her drink into the cup holder, then wedge her popcorn rather roughly into a folded-up seat, and finally toss her purse under the popcorn chair. Then she turned her full attention to the cell phone. From the side of the conversation that Alice could hear, it became quickly obvious that she was waiting for someone, and they were to meet at the movie. The woman had taken off work early to meet this person, who was clearly late. Then she said something that tipped off that she was talking to her daughter.

The mother stormed out of the theater. Alice couldn't help but compare the totally different experiences with the two families sitting near them. The upset mother seemed to have no concern for time or money, yet she had no relationship of value with her child. On the other hand, the father, while perhaps having no surplus cash, had a deep and meaningful relationship with his daughter.

The movie theater dimmed, and previews of upcoming shows began. After about fifteen minutes—actually during the opening credits for the main event—the mother and her daughter came marching in through the doors. Their eyes had not adjusted yet, so they had difficulty getting to their seats. The mother missed her row and motioned her daughter into the chair next to the little girl and her father. Now they were right in front of Alice and her guardian angel, who could hear the frustration in both the mother and her daughter, who were less than quiet. Finally the daughter stated tersely, "Mom, I knew this wouldn't work. Let's just leave. Who cares about this stupid movie?"

"Just shut up and watch—I took time off to do this, so we're going to watch, like it or not!" Shock registered on the little girl who sat next to them—she was having the time of her life and didn't understand.

After a few minutes, the mother remembered she had bought treats and looked to see where they were. She was shocked to see that the man and his daughter next to them were eating the popcorn and had the drink. She leaned over and whispered to her daughter, "That's our popcorn they are eating."

"So what! I'm not hungry anyway." But the mother kept eyeing them as they ate.

The young girl with the dad could hear that the mother next to her was talking about the popcorn. She leaned over to her dad and said, "Daddy, I am going to share our popcorn with these people. I don't think they have the money to buy some for themselves."

"Sure, ask them, but be quiet so we don't disturb anyone."

The little girl reached over, handing her bucket to the girl sitting in the next seat, and asked, "Do you and your mom want some popcorn?"

"No, I am good. Thanks though." However, the mother angrily reached over, "Certainly we want our popcorn." The little girl was taken back but thought to herself, *Wow! She must really be hungry.*

The mother kept the popcorn on her seat and ate slowly. After a few minutes Alice could see the little girl was wondering if she would get the popcorn back when the mother asked if she could have the drink. "Yes, certainly," was the response of this girl as she handed it to the lady. She then whispered to her dad and said, "Daddy, we don't really need those treats anyway; they are not having a good day." She reached over and held her father's hand. The lady kept the drink and the popcorn. This didn't seem to affect the father or daughter at all.

The woman's daughter, too angry with her mother to eat any of her popcorn but apparently getting the munchies, leaned over to her mother and asked if she could go buy some candy. The mother snapped back, "Why don't you ask those two next to us if they want something? My purse is under the seat. Just hurry," she exclaimed. But when the girl reached under the seat, she was unable to find the purse. Boiling over, the mother leaned over her daughter and said to the young girl sitting next to them, "Did you steal my purse as well?"

Shocked, the little girl clasped her father's hand as he said, "I'm sorry, ma'am, but I don't know what you are talking about. Could it possibly be under the seat you had when you came in?"

"What are you talking about?" she snapped back. He kindly pointed to the row in front of them and said, "This is the seat you took originally. Maybe you got confused in the dark and thought you were in the same seats?" he suggested.

The mother looked on the row in front of them and saw her

popcorn and drink, just as she had left them. As she struggled with the realization of what she had done, the guardian angel whispered in Alice's ear.

"Alice, I want you to feel the hearts of both parents here. You probably think that the mother and daughter have less love for each other than the other family, don't you? In fact, I don't think they have liked each other for a long time."

Alice first felt the heart of the mother. "Wow! I didn't expect this, my old friend. This woman loves her daughter with all her heart."

"Yes, she does, Alice. Can you sense what it is she is hoping for?"

Alice concentrated—hard—for a moment before answering. "She realizes that her heightened emotion came as a result of the intensity of her life. She feels as though there is limited time and wants desperately to have a meaningful relationship with her daughter."

"Very good! You are right, and her daughter feels exactly the same way. She too builds frustration on frustration, cycling downward quickly.

"The intense negative emotion was created when the mother felt her daughter didn't care. She desperately wanted to reach out to her daughter today and felt she had exposed her heart and her feelings in making the attempt. When her daughter was late, in order to protect herself from feeling hurt, she became angry and hid behind her frustration. Her raised voice brought a mirrored response from her daughter, ironically for the same reason, and everything then fell apart.

"Typically this woman would have willingly shared and not cared at all about the drink and popcorn. Her false assumption, her sharp criticism, and her selfishness were just an outgrowth of trying to build up rapid defenses around herself as a protection against potential emotional hurt, which stripped her of her common sense. Any hope of finding a solution that would have allowed her to find why her daughter was late faded in the heightened emotion.

"Now go feel the father's heart. How do his feelings and intentions differ?"

"I can tell that he too loves his daughter. And, well, the

security he feels with his daughter's relationship allows him to extend his concern to others. He really wants to help this mother and her daughter find a way to enjoy their time together. He felt that giving them the treats might have helped, but he also wasn't sure if that would somehow add to their frustration."

"You are getting good at this, Alice. You are right about this father—he maintains and builds on his relationship with his daughter, which allows him to teach her invaluable life lessons while dealing with all this intense negative emotion surrounding them.

"Alice, this is very important for you to understand: even though I am helping you to see into the feelings of this mother and father, anyone who keeps his or her emotions in check is able to sense the real feelings of those around them. Because the little girl was secure in her relationship with her father, she sensed that popcorn and a drink were far less important than the need for these other two to feel some positive emotions. If we lose our composure, we become clouded by our own self-interest and place judgment on others. You can see how reacting as the mother has will build toward receiving the same negative response. On the other hand, remaining calm allows for understanding and working through emotional crises to a positive reaction.

"Alice, no matter how intense your feelings are or how strongly others near you are acting, understand that your ability to correct and resolve comes by being sensible. Now let's see how this is all going to end."

As Alice watched, she saw clearly that the mother had now fully recognized her mistake. She handed back both the drink and the remaining popcorn to the generous pair sitting next to her daughter. "I am so sorry," she said. And truly she was embarrassed, as well as humbled, by the young girl's generosity. The lady retrieved her purse from the row in front of her and quickly pulled out double the cost of the treats to give the girl for her misunderstanding. The young girl, however, had no interest in the money and suggested she was happy to share, her father nodding in warm agreement behind her.

This woman had thought the family next to her had stolen, when in fact they had given the "widow's mite." Furthermore, the calm collective response they had given her after her unjust tirade settled her imbalanced emotions, and the mother and her daughter went on to enjoy the movie together. In fact, instead of moving down a row, they asked if they could remain next to the little girl and her father so they could now share their popcorn with them. Alice was amazed at how completely the mood changed in entire theater when these two people set aside their protective walls and warmed up to each other and those around them.

"Well, Alice, I guess this about wraps up our date together this evening. I cannot begin to tell you how much I enjoy getting to know you. We have discussed a lot, haven't we! Now, like the little girl and her popcorn, you must take what has been given to you and share with others, sometimes with those who do not know that they are in need of your help. You will be misjudged and occasionally mistreated, but you must always remember to keep your own emotions in check so that you will be in the position to help. Now let's get you home before your parents wonder what kind of hooligan you've been hanging out with!"

That evening Alice wrote in her journal:

When I become frustrated I will maintain my emotion, realizing that I can only grow by sensing my environment and the people around me accurately. A clear mind will allow me to sustain valuable relationships.

I am honest, generous, patient, virtuous, kind, and even keeled.

The natural being, left free to explore untamed, will tend towards devastation. We must learn restraint regarding physical desires. Discernment of intentions and actions for what they truly are is the pathway to safety and fulfillment.

Chapter 27

One afternoon in early August last year, Alice was hanging out on the school's front lawn while she waited with her friends for their car pool to pick them up. As she looked east toward the mountains of the Wasatch Range, a mental image flashed in her mind of the last time she had hiked to the top of Mount Olympus. Her family had invited a bunch of friends, and they all hiked up together. The weather had been spectacular, everyone had been in great moods, and it had just been one of those perfect days.

One of the things that had made the day so perfect was that her best friend, Sue, had been with them. Now, as they sat in the shade under the aging maple trees surrounding the school lawn, Alice caught Sue's eye and half whispered, "Mount Olympus? Saturday?"

"Perfect! Last time I laughed so hard at your brother I nearly wet my pants! Let's do it!" That night Sue sent out a text to their usual group inviting them on the hike, and by first period the next day, they had positive RSVPs from everyone.

However, as these things tend to do when teenagers get together, by Saturday morning the group had expanded well beyond the few who were invited by Sue's original text. In fact, when Alice and her car load of four (driven by Sue's very cute older brother!) drove up to the trail head parking lot, the lot was nearly full. She was blown away by the number of kids from school who were there, only some of whom she knew. As the girls got out of the car, someone yelled out a challenge that the first one to the top would be crowned king, and the last one would have to eat in the school cafeteria for a week. Immediately several groups took off on a dead run, laughing and taunting each other all the way.

Alice and her group joined some guys whom they knew and

began a more casual ascent, chattering as if they had not seen each other in weeks instead of just a matter of hours. The first third of the trail made its way through grasses and sage brush. Along the way they stopped several times to take in the simple beauty of a single clump of mountain holly or sego lily.

It had been a wetter than normal summer, so the flora along the trail was more notable than usual. All of Alice's group had made the climb several times before and knew that they would have plenty of time at this pace to spend time with the others at the summit and still make it back down before nightfall. Besides, who besides sophomores ever really ate in the cafeteria? It was an empty threat at best, though it did conjure up unpleasant memories of too dry macaroni and processed cheese. And sophomores.

The comfortable chatter of good friends made the hike go quickly. The middle third of the trail was dominated by pine trees as the trail wound its way through a narrow canyon. Before they knew it, their group of eight had emerged from the forest and were making their way up the somewhat barren final third of the trail, until suddenly they were a mere hundred yards from the summit. "What an incredible day!" said Brad. "Warm without being hot, sunny without beating our heads in—this is way better than two-a-days at football practice! Man, am I ever glad that's over."

Nodding her head in the general direction of their destination, Alice smiled ruefully, "Well, we're definitely not the first at the top, and whoever was is having a great time, I would say. Think they're loud enough?"

As they approached the summit itself, Alice's attention was drawn not to the amazing view of the surrounding snow-capped peaks and broad, green valleys but rather to a small group of kids huddled to one side. Instinctively she knew that something was not right. Maybe it was how they huddled protectively around whatever was in the center of their huddle, maybe it was the collective number of tattoos and black-dyed heads, or maybe it was just the aura they projected, but something was definitely not right.

Tradition required that Alice's group walk to the summit one by one, then turn around to give the rest of their group high fives to officially recognize the accomplishment of having hiked to the top of Mount Olympus. And from the vantage point of that elevation, Alice could see clearly into the center of this other group's circle.

An impressive assortment of pills lay spread out on two tie-dyed bandanas. This first group to ascend were clearly intent on achieving other highs than just physical elevation. One of the boys whom she sort of recognized but didn't know well turned toward her and smiled happily, "Hey, guys. Great idea to start the new school year with a little trip to the mountains! Thanks for inviting us. The least we can do is return the favor. C'mon over and share our 'trail mix' with us."

A blonde girl in Daisy Duke shorts and a sports bra joined in, "Yea, really. The view is definitely better with a little help from our friends here!" She gestured towards the bandanas. "What do you say, guys? The first three are on the house to our slow friends who just made it up the hill. Especially you, Alice! We wouldn't have been here without your invitation in the first place."

The group quickly took up the chant, "Alice! Alice! Alice!" She didn't want to offend them and start a ruckus, but she also wanted no part of their offer. And when Brad put his arm around her shoulders and said, "Oh, c'mon, Alice. Be a good sport and come talk to these guys," her heart nearly broke. Confused, she looked to the east just in time to see one of the plentiful hawks that inhabited the surrounding skies fold its wings and go into a full dive towards the valley floor.

"Alice? Is that you?" It was not a voice of one of the friends who had come, yet she recognized it. As she turned around, up the trail walked an older man, aided by a walking stick made out of a tree branch. Though he wore American clothing, the darkened skin and wide-brimmed hat shouted to Alice his true identity.

Sue, who thought she knew everything there was to know about her friend, didn't recognize this newcomer and asked, "Alice, who is that? He's not going to narc on everybody, is he?"

"No, don't worry. He's an old friend of mine. Listen, I'm just going over there for a minute to talk with him. Be right back." But then she looked directly at Sue and said meaningfully, "Listen, you be careful while I'm gone. You're my best friend. I need you to be strong."

As Alice left the combined groups to walk over to her friend, she heard Sue tell those who had teased Alice about not participating in the drugs, "You guys don't know Alice very well. There is no way she'll drop any pills, no matter how hard you push."

What she didn't hear was Brad's bitter chuckle and comment: "Yeah, that is what I used to say too. Hey, Sue, how about you? Have you got the guts to do a little flying now that you don't have Miss Goody Goody holding you down?"

Smiling broadly, Alice approached her friend, "I guess you got permission to visit me again."

"Yes, little one, I am here to give you another piece of wisdom, but your friend Sue needs this information even more than you do. This time on the summit will stand as a turning point in her life. You need to know that one of Sue's guardian angels asked me to put you in a place to help her."

"Oh, I would do anything for Sue. Please tell me what I need to know."

The old monk placed his hand on the back of her elbow and led her over to a large rock overlooking the valley. Alice was surprised at the strength she felt in his frail-looking hands and at the spring in his short but steady stride. "Alice, you have been blessed in your young life to have made some commitments that have resulted from your internal guide, your faith, and your family's beliefs. These decisions have been tested, and you have become strong.

"But just as you have been strengthened by people in your world and mine, so too are there those in both our worlds who would prevent you from achieving what you are here for. Knowing that truth will help you to overcome such evil designs, but I also want to teach you something else that you can share with Sue on the trail down.

"Little one, when we make life choices, there are long-lasting implications that come as a result of our decisions. Let's use this mountain as an example. Would it be out of the question to assume you do not want to fall off this summit and down the face of this beautiful mountain? That's a silly question, right? Nonetheless, some people have fallen from this very location and either been hurt or killed. If you had committed in your heart to never fall off a mountain, what would you do to ensure that would never happen?"

"Well, I would stay well back from the edge, just like we are now."

"Exactly! You have just said an important truth, for you have a good sense of how far you can go. Those who know their limits and refrain from testing them will remain safe; however, those who have not yet established their limits are free to be enticed into exceeding where the boundaries should have been.

"Not long ago a young man fell to his death off the face of this mountain. Some people think his death was caused by a single mistake, but it was actually the result of years of poor decision making. The first time he hiked up here he was scared to death of the edge and stayed where we are here on this rock. From here we can observe the danger without falling victim to it. The next time he came up here it was with some young kids who had learned of the thrill and excitement of testing their limits and experimented by stepping out to that little outcropping right there."

"Yes, I have seen people stand out there before. It seems dangerous, but it is not always deadly for I have never seen any of them fall."

"Perhaps you are right, Alice—this group of young men left the mountain safe on that trip, but every time they came up together after that they would challenge nature a little more and move closer to the edge. The margin of safety grew ever smaller. On the day of this young man's fatal fall, his heart was clearly telling him he was pushing beyond safe limits, but his head and his ego suggested that his previous experiments had had no negative consequences, so neither would this experience. He recognized his error too late. His friends sobbed for hours here on top of this summit, at last understanding the consequences for having not respected the laws of nature. Each young man had a life experience—and one had a death experience—that was completely unnecessary.

"You see, my dear Alice, life provides many situations where there is no room for compromise: one step in the wrong direction can lead to disaster. At the time it may appear to be just one step, but each time the situation arises we take just more step beyond the last one. Very few people walk to the edge of a precipice the first time they see it and then stepping right over the edge. Instead, we test with little steps, each time removing a bit of our guard and weakening any commitment to safety. Before we realize it, we have stepped to far out onto a slippery slope from which there is no rescue."

The old man went silent and looked off in the distance, as if listening to someone only he could see. After several seconds, he closed his eyes, nodded, and turned back to look gently into his young friend's eyes. "Alice, up to this point, we have talked about the message that Sue's guardian angel wanted me to pass on to you. Now it is my turn. What I want you to understand is that when you make a pledge to yourself of what you will and will not do in life, you need to remain dedicated to this promise. As you do, it will become easier and those around you will support you in your commitment. Did you notice that your friends knew you would not even entertain for a minute the thought of accepting drugs from those other kids. Your spirit of commitment allowed them to gain strength.

"Here is the secret to great power in making commitments: no one is perfect. By understanding this, we can surround ourselves with others who share similar bonds. When we have a moment of weakness, these friends will support us. If we take a step off our track, they will be there to pull us back on. It is never too late."

"But why does Alice need a message? She is my best friend and one of my biggest supporters!"

"Ah, my little one. Your innocence may surprise me at times, but it never disappoints me! When you left, Sue resisted experimenting with the pills that she was offered for free. But she did try smoking marijuana. Now she feels bad, and she needs you. If you share with her your wisdom, she can get back on track. She will have help from my part of the world, but she must have your support as well if she is to survive this test. Although she does not fully recognize it, she has begun the slide to a life of difficulty, which will be very hard to correct. She is still at the top of her slippery slope, but you must know that if she does not stop now and return to who she really is, her problems will not end with drugs but may include stepping out on her spouse, taking advantage of her employer, and hurting many loved ones—and many more innocent bystanders. She will begin a life of lying, cheating, stealing, spreading falsehoods behind others' backs, and showing unjustified prejudice. These will all lead to great pain if she does not correct her path.

"Go now—we will see each other again soon. Support and share your wisdom with Sue. She needs you more than she knows!"

"Hold it! How will I know what to say? What if I can't do this right? I don't want my best friend to become a divorced, drug-addict convict with a suicide wish if I don't say exactly the right thing!"

Gently he placed his slender hand on her shoulder. "Do you feel that? Not on your shoulder—in your heart?" Alice nodded as a tingling clarity and peace began somewhere in the middle of her torso and moved outward. "That is your gift—and your responsibility. You need not worry what to say or do. When the time is right, you will know. That is who you are, Alice. It has been your destiny since before you were born. You have only to accept your identity and embrace it with all your heart. Choose not to do so, and I will have to turn to another to change the world!" His eyes twinkled with life and love for his student.

With mock exasperation, Alice threw her hands in the air and moaned, "Okay, I'll do my part, but I refuse to wear any kind of superhero costume. That's where I draw the line!" And off she went in search of her best friend—and world domination, if that's what it was going to take.

"Hey, Sue, what's up? What do you say we get going down!" Alice looked around. "Thanks for waiting for me. It looks like the others in our group are just heading out too, huh?"

Sue wished in her heart that Alice had not disappeared and knew there was no way she could let Alice know she had smoked weed while she was gone. Maybe if she turned the conversation back to Alice, she wouldn't have to say anything about what she had done. "Hey, where did you go anyway? You were gone quite awhile!"

"Yeah, sorry about that. Remember that old friend of mine that we saw? We were just catching up on a few things."

"Oh, yeah? Like what? Tell me about it."

"You know—a bit of this, a bit of that. Nothing really. We probably should get on the trail—I didn't bring a flashlight, and the sun does set a little earlier each night. Let's get going."

As they walked down the mountain together, Alice intentionally walked a bit slowly so the others would get far enough away that the two could talk openly. When the gap appeared to be adequate, Alice figured it was time to get down to business. "So, how did things go after I left to go visit with my friend? I mean, you know I decided long ago to never enter the path of drugs and what not, but how did the rest of our group do? If ever there was a time to experiment, this would seem to be a good one—free drugs, no adults, quite a ways from home. I could see how someone could falter in a situation like this?"

Sue choked on her answer, then cleared her throat and tried again. Although she spoke clearly enough, Alice knew her far too well to not recognize her discomfort. "Not much, really. When they saw that we were all pulling an Alice Callister on them, they quit trying. We just hung out with them and talked—you know, they were really a decent bunch of kids once you got to know them a bit. I think they use just to loosen up a bit so they can see life from a different perspective."

"So they didn't pressure you guys any more after I left? As hard as they were pushing me, I would have thought they would keep in up after I left."

"Well, I guess they did offer some other stuff besides the pills if anyone wanted to experiment, but I can't say for sure how hard they pressured anyone."

"So, tell me Sue, did anyone do anything that perhaps you wish hadn't happened?"

"Not that I am aware of," answered Sue with a sidelong glance at Alice. "They brought out some weed shortly after you left and passed that around. I didn't pay a lot of attention to what others were doing. I mean, it would have been pretty easy to take a toke without anyone seeing. Know what I mean?"

"Whew! That's good to know, Sue. I mean, part of me was really hoping that all of you had stayed true to your convictions, and part of me was curious because of how dangerous it might be driving down the canyon next to someone who's a bit high for the first time and doesn't know how to handle driving while under the influence of alcohol, drugs, or both.

Alice felt a peaceful surge, beginning somewhere around her heart, and decided to forge ahead. "There's something else that I want to say, Sue. I know that none of us is able to be perfect all the time; that's one reason why it's so important to have friends who understand and support us until we can be stronger. I'm starting to see something that my mother has often said, although don't tell her that I'm saying this: we don't realize how little decisions can change our life course and lead us to places we never wanted to go. One step becomes two, then three, and soon we are off and moving so fast it is hard to get back. I think that at first we move so little or so gradually that we miss the fact we are even off track. Then when we realize our path has changed, we are quick to make excuses.

"For example, Sue, you said that those guys pulled out some weed after I left. What if I had stayed and taken a smoke when it was offered. I mean, sometimes I wonder what that would feel like, if it would really relieve a bit of the pressure. But I'm afraid that I might like what I felt, and next time it would be easier when I felt stressed to smoke an entire joint. Who knows where it could lead after that? I'd be stupid to think that I'm immune to straying. It is so much easier to make decisions before choices are presented so there is no wiggle room and we are quick to maintain our chosen paths."

Sue stopped on the path and pulled Alice around to look at her full on. Tears ran down her cheeks as she said, "Alice, I am so ashamed. I can't lie to my best friend—I did take a few puffs. Honestly, it was sort of a rush, but it was also so nasty that I can't imagine ever doing that again."

"We've been friends since kindergarten, Sue. I knew inside what you had done. I also know that you know your decision was wrong, but we can learn something from it. You now see how easy it would be to fall into doing things that are not only offensive to who you are but that also lead to habits you may not be able to correct. It might not seem like that after just a couple of puffs, but it is easier than we both realize. Knowing this puts strength in conviction. Let's both realize that this was wrong and even crazy, but it will give us power to never do it again."

Sue threw her arms around her friend and sobbed, "Oh, Alice thank you. I hurt so bad inside right now."

"This might sound a bit harsh, but Sue, that pain can become covered over time with excuses. Realizing, admitting, correcting, and asking for support will stop this sidetrack right now. Sue, I love you and am here for you. I forgive you; now forgive yourself. There will be a time when I need your support—let's commit to being there always for each other."

As the two came off the mountain, each had been blessed with new wisdom. Alice knew that Sue had help from the other side and that the experiences of the day perhaps in some small way kept her friend on her life course toward goodness.

That night, Alice made this brief entry in her journal:

I follow my heart, knowing it won't fail me. When others are in need, I will help, understanding that I too may need their support.

I am honest, generous, patient, virtuous, kind, even keeled, and perceptive.

Our ability to understand and reason will prove invaluable, navigating us down paths of success, allowing our ability to accomplish anything. It isn't necessary for us to live through all experiences to learn; others can teach us, and they do so willingly.

Chapter 28

"Alice, what I want to share tonight is the importance of education. At your age you may think, 'I can't wait until I finish school and no longer have to study.' Right?"

"True story, Guardian Angel." Alice was no longer intimidated by being visited by an angel in the middle of the night, and this evening she was feeling just a bit flippant, despite her efforts to be serious. It had been a great day, and her spirits were still soaring.

"Learning is one of the greatest gifts we have as human beings. You need to think for a minute about the capacity you have in your mind. Picture yourself and what your brain is doing for you—let's start with a dream.

"Do you remember the last dream you had?"

"Yes, silly, it was with you! Aren't you angels supposed to know mysteries and all that stuff? How can you do that if you can't remember what happened two nights ago?"

"Okay, good point. Go to one before that for me—a different one please."

Though the old monk showed nothing but patience for her giddiness, Alice could tell that he had something important to share with her. Taking a deep breath, she thought a moment and then answered, this time seriously. "Well, a while ago I was scheduled to give a talk in front of several hundred people, and was quite nervous about it. I hadn't yet put together ideas on what I was going to cover. One night I found myself giving the talk; I must say, I hit it out of the park, even though it was just a dream.

"I rattled off things in my speech that I didn't even know I knew. I pictured every detail, including the audience and what they were doing. I felt the emotion of every moment—crying, laughing, and caring. It was amazing I must admit. I remember waking up thinking, 'That was the best speech I ever heard, and it was only a dream!'

"I immediately went over to my desk to write the details so I wouldn't forget: I felt truly inspired."

"That is a good example, Alice. Think of the power of your mind when it is clear to think without limitations. Dreams have detail, such as color, emotion, sense, and understanding. Most dreams are simply the result of your brain accessing your experiences and placing them in order. You are seeing what can be, perhaps through inspiration.

"Now think of the greatest computer ever designed and the amazing capacity it holds. Aren't you shocked by what a computer can do today?"

"Totally! I had to read an article about that for my science class the other day, and I was amazed at what those big supercomputers can do and how fast they can calculate incredible things. I wish I could retain that much information and think that fast."

"Well, Alice, actually computers pale in comparison to what your mind can do. You are operating a body, providing it with life-sustaining precision while processing mobility, understanding, and memory—all at the same time.

"You have stored amazing technical information and have recall instantly when needed. I can sit here with you and suggest different times in your life, and you will have recall with emotion. I can ask you about someone in your life, and you will have not only a picture in your mind but a recollection of your interaction with them as well.

"Things you have learned are sometimes slow to return but are there for you when needed. Your reactions are instant, and your ability to multi-task unmatched by any other living species on the planet. There is no computer as impressive as our minds, and there will never be one that will hold a candle to what we can do with our mind.

"Alice, many have written about the power of the mind and suggest that 'we are what we think.' The power of the mind enables us in all we do. When you master this principle, nothing will stop you from becoming what and who you want to become. If you think you are smart, talented, or athletic, you are.

What your mind believes becomes your reality. You can and will accomplish anything, especially if that thing has positive value.

"My young student, gain an appreciation of this great tool and use it to its full potential. Through learning, you open doors to improving your surroundings. If you sit down with your grandparents and ask them about their world when they were children compared with today, you will be shocked at what advancements we have gained.

"You see, knowledge builds on itself—your knowledge gives you understanding, and your understanding allows you to see your purpose. As you discover your purpose, you unlock unlimited potential.

"If you will spend your life with a thirst for knowledge, learning, and seeking education from a variety of sources, you will develop a deep understanding of life. This understanding is wisdom.

"Wisdom comes to us in a variety of methods. One way is gaining knowledge and experience by learning life-lessons first hand. This understanding of wisdom is deeply rooted in our psyche as it comes with direct and personal emotion. Learning wisdom by experience is the most difficult method, but sometimes we have to learn life-lessons the hard way—through painful consequences.

"Another way to gain wisdom is through watching others and learning from their experiences. The advantage of this method over direct experience is that you do not have to learn as many difficult lessons. You will have more time to pursue positive life paths.

"The best method may be the one most difficult to master. It is intuitive discernment by reflection. At this level one can put together life-lessons or experiences and observations of others to gain an understanding of anticipated outcomes.

"Those who can master wisdom at this level are rare and of great worth to each of us. These individuals are ones you should seek after, hoping to glean some of their understanding.

"By obtaining wisdom, our lives benefit since growth is gained at a much quicker pace. We are blessed with greater discernment, making our joys in life long-lasting and more completely expressed within our souls. We are capable of participating in the improvement of society as we have knowledge of the big picture.

"Our sincerity gives others an example, opening doors for our influence as others begin to solicit our observations. As we participate in the growth of others, our wisdom is magnified and we begin to master the highest level of wisdom.

"Alice, no matter your age, regardless of your experience, regardless of your understanding, you will always do well to seek out the knowledge of your fellow beings. Learn from your own experiences, make observations of others, but be wise enough to listen to and evaluate another's opinion for its real value.

"Seek out those who love you, those who have your best interest at heart, and those who are trusted advisors. Know your path to any desired outcome is quicker and easier by asking someone who has taken the same route or who has gained an understanding through experience and personal knowledge."

The guardian angel reached out to Alice and took her hand. "We will take a quick tour tonight as our time is limited, but you may find the feelings to be very intense. I want you to feel the instant impression developed by someone who has reached a point of discernment through learning."

Alice recognized from watching news broadcasts that they were looking at somewhere in the Middle East, probably Iraq. A small platoon of American soldiers was making its way through rough terrain, stealthily approaching the outskirts of a small village. Her attention was drawn to one soldier in particular—there was nothing special about how he moved or looked, she was just drawn to watch his movements carefully.

"That's right, Alice," her guardian angel whispered in her left ear. "The young man you are watching will be the focal point of this experience. Play close attention now!"

Though the sun had not yet risen over the rocky terrain to the east, the coming glow was sufficient to enable the young men to carefully pick out their path. Alice could see that this site had been used for military purposes before. Empty shell casings lay about the earth in random small piles, and natural outcroppings that could serve as cover were pockmarked from having been shot at while soldiers hid carefully behind it. Alice's soldier stepped carefully over a small log in his path and continued on.

As he did so, he unknowingly narrowly missed stepping on an IED, or improvised explosive device. Fifteen feet behind him, however, as the next soldier in line stepped over the same log, he came down directly on the trigger for the device, setting it off.

Though Alice's soldier was a full five yards away when the small bomb went off, the impact was immediate and his pain more intense than anything he could describe. He knew only when he came to was that he was in a different place. He couldn't help but think, "Is this what dying feels like?"

The next thing he was conscious of was a familiar groan behind him. Looking over his shoulder he saw what looked like his friend lying on the ground. The soldier rubbed his eyes—where was the lower half of his body? *I must be hallucinating—this makes no sense at all.* Pain rippled through his shoulder. *Well, I must be alive, 'cause this sure isn't heaven!* Rubbing his eyes, he looked again with every sense he could muster. Suddenly his eyes focused, his mind cleared, and immediately his reflexes kicked in. That was his friend, no doubt about it.

Pushing his own pain to the background, he jumped up and lunged forward. Not everything seemed to be working exactly right, but he didn't have time to figure it all out. Everything was in disarray; nothing made sense at all. What was part of their world just a minute before was now gone. The one bit of clarity to it all was that he knew that he was his friend's only hope.

Instinct kicked in—years of training were paying off. The soldier in front of him was missing both legs, and the life blood he so desperately needed was rushing out of the torn and jagged stumps. In minutes, maybe seconds, he would pass the point of no return, and his life would be over.

He ripped the field pack from his back and tore open the first tourniquet. The blood made his work slippery, but he seemed to have divine help as he applied the wrap in record time. Then he snatched at the second package, with similar results. Though his eyes seemed to see in slow motion, he knew his hands had never worked so quickly. Once the tourniquets were secured, he ripped open a bag of QuikClot and sprinkled the contents liberally where legs should have been, and were five minutes before. With the most obvious injuries taken care of, he quickly scanned his friend for additional injuries: though cut up a bit and in incredible pain, the wounded man had suffered no other life-threatening damage.

After waiting for the gunfire to subside, the soldier picked his friend up from the pool of blood and carried him to safety. Within moments, a medical helicopter was bearing him off to the nearest field hospital, where skilled doctors would do everything in their power to preserve both his life and his quality of living.

Alice was exhausted from feeling the intensity of the experience—the pain, the fear, the uncertainty, and the tremendous love that this young soldier had for his friend. She closed her eyes, held her face in her hands, and quietly wept.

"Alice, this young man saved the life of his friend and comrade on this horrible day. He was awarded with a medal of honor and recognized for saving this soldier in record time. But that is but a precursor to what I really want you to experience. Watch as we move to the ceremony at which the soldier received his medal. In case you can't tell, the woman in the navy blue dress is our soldier's mother. I want you to look deep into her heart, Alice, and feel what is there as her son receives his award.

Alice found herself in a rather official looking room, too well appointed to be a work area but not so large as to be able to handle large assemblies. Seating was in place for perhaps a hundred people at best. The United States flag was posted at the front of the room on the left side, next to the official flag of the United States Marine Corps. Two television cameras recorded the event, and nearly a dozen reporters occupied the third and fourth rows of seating on the right side of the room. On the front row were seated a family, probably belonging to the soldier receiving the award, and though the action was taking place at the front of the room where the ceremony was taking place, Alice focused all her attention on the woman in the navy blue dress.

The first thing Alice noticed was the clarity of her eyes. They truly acted as the window to her deep and expressive soul. As tears entered her eyes, they took on a brilliant shimmering glow, at once magical and revelatory in their expressiveness. No longer was there a physical appearance but rather a clear radiant projection into eternity. Alice could see directly into her soul, could feel the beat of her heart!

The guardian angel spoke softly, "Consider, Alice, who gives more serving your country? The brave men and women who are willingly giving the ultimate sacrifice? Was it the young man who lost his legs? This fine soldier who saved his life? Perhaps, but feel the heart of this mother.

"Fully engaged in the life of her children, she knows without question that her son is doing what he wants, what he believes, what is necessary. He will sacrifice all if required, knowing it is his duty, sensing it is what he was born to do. She lives for nothing more than to know of his safety. Combat and all that comes with it are a part of their lives now.

"This woman lives every day with two objectives. First, she awakes every morning and offers words of prayer for the safety of those who have dedicated their lives to protect hers and lives like hers across the entire nation.

"Second, as she retires to bed each night, she thanks Deity that another day has passed without the 'black car' pulling into the driveway and delivering bad news from the field."

Alice responded reverently: "We praise and honor those who serve our country. We pray for their safety and well-being. We know with certainty that it is our freedoms they protect. For me, I know now, after looking into the soul of a mother; there are some who give more. They, the mothers, might argue differently for the sake of their children in the services, but I know better.

"To the mothers of our service men and women, we must say 'Thank you!' We pray with you for the protection of your children and for your peace and safety, hoping your rewards in life will be all that you yearn for.

"I personally acknowledge you for giving more than I could give, more than I had known possible, and more than what has been described as 'the ultimate sacrifice.'

"I know that mothers will remain noble, so may peace, comfort, and understanding be theirs. Let those they have brought into the world receive recognition, love and respect. May the hope and inspiration we receive from you be given back tenfold; may we always recognize that it is we who have benefited through your gift."

Through her tears, Alice heard her guardian angel say softly,

"Little one, never be too old, too smart, or too stubborn to see wisdom." And then her alarm went off, telling her it was time to get up for school. As she opened her eyes, she noticed she was covered with sweat from the torrent of emotions she had just experienced.

Quickly she went to her desk to jot down her feelings and what she learned:

I have unlimited potential, and as a result I will seek learning all my life. My education will come from many sources, so I will observe openly.

I am honest, generous, patient, virtuous, kind, even keeled, perceptive, and wise.

We must maintain an active spirit in all we do. The mind functions such that whatever is thought is lived. Build strength and vitality in life; the energy will carry us to greatness.

Chapter 29

Dust. Wind. Wind blowing dust. Or was it the dust that was carrying the wind with its movement?

All Alice really knew was that she had had more of each in the past two days than she remembered in all the rest of her days on this earth. An earth made of dust and wind, of course. It was inevitable.

It had started two days ago at three-thirty in the morning when her father stuck his head in the doorway to roust her out of bed. She would have a long day ahead of her, and Jim wanted to make sure that she didn't miss any of it. Her mother had helped her pack for the trip last night, but mornings always belonged to her dad—especially if they were early. He claimed that early morning swimming practice had trained him to arise early: Alice was convinced it was just a cancerous gene, one that she fortunately had not inherited. "I'll have breakfast ready in five minutes, honey. Can't be late this morning!"

"Oh, for the love, Dad! On what morning have you ever let us be late for anything? This one is just particularly early!" Despite her protests, which she did mostly just to see how her father would react, she was quite excited for this day to arrive. She had signed up for this experience several months ago when she heard about it. Living in the West, she had heard of the early frontier days and had actually gone to several historical sites honoring the early settlers, such as Fort Bridger, an important supply spot on the Oregon Trail; Hole in the Wall, where outlaws such as Jesse James and Butch Cassidy hung out; and the famous Temple Square in Salt Lake City, where thousands of Mormons escaping persecution in the East settled to pursue religious freedom.

This particular morning was tied in with some of the earliest of the Western-bound pioneers who made the long trek across the Great Plains pulling handcarts rather than wagons. All the youth involved would bus to a location in Wyoming where the pioneers had experienced particular hardship, leaving behind anything that reminded them of modern conveniences. The organizers of the camp had handcarts for the kids to put belongings in and provisions designed to be similar to what the people had while traveling. The trek consisted of a 16-mile three-day pull across an area where a handcart company had been caught in a snow storm and many had died. Alice knew from her family's experience in Cambodia and her monk's regular tutelage that not all holidays need be spent at a theme park or on the beach. From what she had heard, this experience could be quite difficult, but meeting its demands successfully would be satisfying physically and spiritually.

To better appreciate what the early pioneers dealt with, the youth who signed up for this trek were first required to make or buy their own clothing from thrift stores. For boys, that meant flannel shirts, cotton pants, and a cheap straw cowboy hat or floppy hillbilly hat. For girls, full-length cotton dresses, bloomers, and a bonnet to protect their heads from sun burn. Alice had sewn her own clothes, being unable to find what she needed elsewhere, which was quite an experience itself. It had been frustrating at times, but when it was all said and done and she stood in front of her bedroom mirror wearing period clothing that she herself had made, she felt pretty darn good. And now, as she slipped into this very dress and donned the bonnet, she couldn't help but feel the beginnings of a kinship with the pioneers. She was very grateful, however, that the leaders of this "youth trek" allowed and even encouraged modern quality footwear instead of making her own!

As Jim drove Alice to the school parking lot where the buses awaited, he felt impressed to share something with her. "Alice, I don't think I shared this with you yet, but since you decided to go on this pioneer trek, I've been doing a little reading study—both about the pioneers and about our own family. I knew that we've been here in the West for several generations now, but I didn't know much more. The other day I found the name of one of your great-great-grandmothers, Rene Callister, on a list of handcart pioneers. It wasn't the same group that had such a hard time in Wyoming that you're going to talk about, but she still went through the experience of helping to pull a handcart with all her family's possessions all the way from the Mississippi River to the Great Basin."

Alice was suddenly less sleepy, knowing that she had a personal tie to what she was going to experience. "Really, Dad? That is so cool! Was she married? How many kids did she have? I wonder if my dress is the same color as hers. Wouldn't that be awesome? I'll bet it was."

"Alice, honey, I really don't know about the dress. All I found was her name on a list. But she wasn't married. She came from Denmark with her parents and her older brother and sister. A note with the list said that she was six years old when they reached their destination, and that disease had taken the lives of her mother and her siblings on the way. Only she and her father survived the trip. I don't know much else."

"How sad! I mean, I love you and all, but if suddenly the rest of the family were gone, well, that would really stink! You know what I mean?"

"Yes, Alice, I do. Helps you appreciate our modern conveniences and lifestyle, doesn't it?" Jim pulled into the parking lot of the school to see that they were among the first to arrive. Two travel buses were waiting, along with a handful of adults going over last-minute checklists and a small group of sleepy teenagers, too tired to talk much.

"Really. Hey, Dad, thanks for telling me. I'm going to think about her the whole time I'm pulling that wonderful cart. Maybe she can inspire me to survive. Well, I see Sue's dad just pulled in with her, so I guess I'll go find a seat on the bus with her. If I'm not back in three days, make sure that my name is on a list so my great-great-grandchildren can know I existed."

"Um, Alice?"

"Yes, Dad?"

"If you don't make it back, you're probably not going to have any children, let alone great-great-grandchildren."

"Good point, Dad. Love you."

"You too, Alice. See you in three days. And don't forget to write in your journal."

The bus ride had been less than memorable, mostly because

all the kids were either sound asleep or trying their very best to slip into that blessed state. A quick stop in Evanston allowed the group to find relief in the gas station's rest stop and purchase a snack. Breakfast at 3:30 a.m. does not last long in a teenage metabolism! Then it was back on the bus and off to Martin's Cove.

A few hours later, the buses began slowing, and the leaders of the trek stood and began giving the group their agenda. "Good morning to you all! In a few minutes, our buses will pull into a parking lot and we will be able to get off and stretch our legs. While you are doing so, please find the couple who will function as your 'pioneer parents' for the next three days. Our families will be larger than the actual pioneer families were, but we haven't had two months of practice pulling handcarts as they did. So we'll make all the families bigger so we have plenty of help in both pushing and pulling. Once your family is all together, you will all place your gear in your family handcart, and your parents will lead you out on the trail heading into the mountains. Our first day's pull is fairly light, so we'll only be going about four miles before nightfall."

"Alice!" Sue whispered.

"Hmmm?"

"We're in the middle of nowhere."

"T'would appear so."

"Alice?"

"Hmmm?"

"If I die out here, throw me in the cart and bring my body home, would you? I think I saw a wolf a minute ago."

"Sure thing, Sue. Sure thing. And good luck with your new family, just in case you happen to live. I'm sure I'll see you when we stop this evening."

Soon the buses pulled into the parking lot, everyone unloaded, and with the usual relative chaos the families were all formed up and gathered around their assigned handcarts. Alice's parents helped their new kids load their personal bags into the cart, along with the food supplies that each family had been given, so that the load was equally distributed on the cart.

The carts themselves were fairly simple in terms of engineering—two wheels about three feet in diameter connected by a single axle, a wooden box sat on top of the axle and measured four feet square with twelve-inch high sides, and a wooden trace in front of the box into which two people at a time could step in order to push the front bar and thus pull the cart forward. People could also push the cart from behind or help to pull it forward by tugging on short ropes attached to the front corners of the cart. Whoever was not pushing, pulling, or tugging would walk alongside or behind the cart—a task that could prove fairly strenuous in itself due to the long skirts, blowing winds, and extreme weather.

The carts used on this modern trek had iron wheels, but the original carts used wooden wheels bound with rawhide. One of the major problems the pioneers had with the carts was that the wheels were sometimes built in haste using green wood that had not properly cured in the wheel shape, so as they traveled the wheel could splinter, crack, and come apart as it dried under the abuse of day-to-day travel.

Into the box went their food, sleeping bags, and duffel bags with changes of clothing. Alice marveled that families could even begin to reduce their household belongings down to what would fit into that space, but she also understood the need to keep the weight to a minimum. The pioneers also had to find a way to place children too young to walk and the ill or infirm on the cart with their food and belongings. Before taking a single step, she had a greater appreciation for what these courageous settlers had accomplished.

When the cart was packed and properly balanced, the family gathered around the cart for some last-minute information and instruction. "Dad" Olsen spoke first: "We're very excited to have you all with us in our family on this youth trek. We are absolutely convinced that this will be very rewarding, very challenging, and very memorable to each one of you. To help you feel a connection to the pioneers whom we are honoring with this experience, Mom is handing out to each of you a name. This name belongs to one of the original members of the Martin or Willey handcart company. We have tried hard to match you up with someone who is approximately the same age on their trek as you are now. We weren't able to be exact, but the assignments should be relatively close."

Mom finished handing out the names on 3 x 5 cards. On the front was the name in bold, black letters, and on the back was a four- to six-sentence description of the person. Her heart skipped a beat as she read aloud, "Emily Wall." She turned the card over. "Emily Wall was 16 years old when she left England to travel to Zion. She was the second of nine children. The Wall family could not afford to emigrate together, so they sent Emily and her older brother, Joseph (age 17), to travel ahead of them. After Joseph nearly drowned while crossing a river, he became very ill, and Emily had to pull him in the handcart for several days with only the help of a young girl. Emily Wall typified pioneer faith and courage."

"Okay, Olsen family," Dad called cheerily. "It's time to hit the trail. Steve and Alice, why don't you take the first turn at the crossbar in front of the cart, and the rest of us will help to push on the back of the cart and to pull on the ropes." And off they went on the first leg of their handcart pull.

As they walked, Alice tried hard to think of her great-grandmother and how she might have dealt with the challenge of pulling the cart. But the winds of the high plains of Wyoming were blowing consistently if not hard. Dust flew into her hair, her mouth, her ears, and her eyes. The sun pounded down on them as if that were its only job, and judging from the little vegetation that surrounded them, there seemed precious little else for the sun to do. It certainly wasn't preoccupied with making things green!

After four miles of dust and sweat and heat (though Alice's feet claimed they had gone a full fifteen!), the group pulled their carts into a circle and began to set up camp. Mom and Dad Olsen helped put together a quick meal based cooked in an open dutch oven over a small open fire—small chunks of beef, some broth, a few carrots, and a hard tack roll for each. It was meager, but they were so tired that it seemed heavenly. After cleaning up the pots and their eating utensils, all the families gathered together around a central fire, where the leaders told several inspirational stories of the pioneers, led the group in three of the better known pioneer songs, and then sent everyone off to sleep.

Alice was not sure how the pioneers slept, but she was pretty sure they stayed together in their families. Sleeping arrangements was one area in which the youth trek differed, for the handcarts were lined up in a long line on the trail, with the boys sleeping on one side of the trail and the girls on the other. Alice barely had enough energy to find Sue and chat briefly with her before rolling out her sleeping pad and bag under the starry sky and climbing inside. Judging from the immediate sounds of heavy breathing and snoring all about her, she was not alone in her total mental and physical exhaustion.

Before sunrise the next morning, her new parents rousted them all out of bed and the families reassembled get small cooking fires prepared. They made flour biscuits, which they had with a little honey dribbled over them and washed down with cold water. Alice had never had such tasty biscuits, she was convinced! Again, it left her a bit wanting, but they had to ration their food supply carefully—everything they had for food was right there on the handcart with their personal bags and sleeping gear.

After breakfast, they cleaned up, packed up, and lined up to begin the day's pull. Alice's hands were stiff and sore from pushing against the bar, as were her calves and shoulders, but fifteen minutes of travel did wonders to loosen her muscles up. Because the action of pushing and pulling was simple mechanics, her mind was left to wander wherever she wanted, and she found herself thinking of her great-grandmother, who had left Denmark at such an early age and was traveling the plains under far more difficult circumstances than Alice herself. She wondered what thoughts her youthful ancestor must have had, and suddenly realized that, in the end, she was a little girl and must have sang songs, thought of games and dolls, and maybe dreamed of having enough to eat and what her mother might have cooked for dinner back in Denmark. Suddenly she realized that she had been humming the words to a pioneer song that they had learned last night, and couldn't help but sing softly to herself:

Put your shoulder to the wheel, push along,
Do your duty with a heart full of song.
We all have work; let no one shirk.
Put your shoulder to the wheel, push along.

By the second line, Mom and Dad Olsen had joined her in singing, then the rest of her temporary family joined in. After they finished what they knew, Alice turned to another, and soon the entire train of handcart families were singing in unison:

And should we die before our journey's through,
Happy day! All is well!
We then are free from toil and sorry, too;
With the just we shall dwell!
But if our lives are spared again,
To see the Saints their rest obtain,
Oh, how we'll make this chorus swell—
All is well! All is well!

The singing in the morning air helped the time go by, and within an hour from the time they had started, the train found themselves coming to a small river. There was no way around, and no ferry to take them across, so everyone just grabbed onto their cart and headed across the shallow ford. At its deepest, it ran no more than eighteen inches, but the current was swift and occasionally someone would lose footing and end up in the drink. With the temperature rising already, the cool water actually felt quite good, but the leaders soberly reminded the trek participants that the handcart company whose names they each carried with them came through in the bitter cold of an early winter. Many had poor or no shoes at all, having worn them out on the extended pull across the Great Plains. Without proper means to dry themselves and then place warm, dry shoes and socks on, frostbite took its toll, and more than a few of the original pioneers eventually lost toes or more because of the need to cross this river in the freezing cold.

After the river was forded by all, the next challenge was a very steep hill. No one was singing now. Every ounce of strength, every tiny bit of breath was reserved for forcing their handcart against the gravity and steepness of the hill. Large rocks in the trail meant that momentum was difficult to maintain as step by step they groaned their way up the trail. To make matters worse, the wind had returned, bringing with it its partner—incessant dust. At times Alice wondered whether they would make it to the top, but each time some member of the family would murmur a word of encouragement, a compliment, or occasionally a lighthearted comment that they somehow dragged out of their spirits to share and thus lighten their collective load. She also found a hardened will in thinking of Emily Wall, pulling her desperately ill brother essentially by herself for mile after mile in these conditions.

Eventually they did arrive at the top, and the leaders determined that here would be a good place for a rest and a bit of lunch—biscuits, jerky, and good long drinks of water. Each participant knew that while there was a general attempt to eat similar foods to what the pioneers had eaten, their leaders made very certain that they did not dehydrate or go hungry, as had the original pioneers. By the time they reached this point in the journey, the pioneers of the Martin and Willey handcart companies were restricted to but a few ounces of flour per day and most of their water came from the snow they melted! Alice might not have had all that she wanted, but she knew she would not suffer either.

After lunch, they proceeded on up the trail, soon arriving at the area after which the memorial site was named—Martin's Cove. While awaiting a rescue team from the Great Salt Lake Valley, dozens of starving, nearly frozen people sought refuge from the snow and bitter cold in this natural cove against the foothills. Some died; others were not so fortunate. The modern trek leaders asked the youth on this trek to walk into and through this area as individuals rather than groups, all maintaining their silence out of reverence for the sacredness of the site, made holy through the sacrifice of life and love. As Alice walked along the path, occasionally stopping to read memorial plaques that told the story of the original pioneers, she felt drawn sit on a large rock just off the trail, next to a place where a mother had buried her newborn baby, unable to sustain her young life in such extreme circumstances.

So there she sat—alone in the heat and the dust and the constant wind of the high plains of Wyoming, alone in her sweat-drenched pioneer clothing that she had made with her own hands, alone in this place that felt and smelled of life and yet was so dominated by the sense of death and suffering. Yet she was not alone, for all around her she sensed the presence of those who had been there before, whose bodies had been left behind when the rescuers came at last, whose names were now carried by two busloads of teenagers seeking to understand the past and themselves. And as she sat there alone and yet not alone, she sensed another presence, both ancient and familiar, and she smiled through the combined salt of her tears and of her sweat.

"Hello, Alice."

"Hello, Guardian Angel. I wondered if I might see you here."

"Do you remember when I first visited you at night in your home? I told you that I had given you the bracelet in a sacred place, one that I had access to? And I also told you that you would find other sacred places during your life? This, little one, is one of those places. It has been made sacred by the faith and courage of those who passed through here and those who passed on here—and by the faith of those who continue to come here."

"I have to admit that there were times when I didn't think I would make it—and I haven't had anything to deal with compared to the pioneers!"

"No, Alice, you haven't. But you have learned some of the same principles here, have you not? And after that, it is simply a matter of conviction and understanding those principles more completely, not learning them anew."

"What principles do you speak of, my wise friend? Help me to see what you mean?"

"You have learned that the pioneers had very little with them. They left many things in their European homes, and the trail across the plains is marked by unnecessary items that were discarded to lighten the load they had to push. What have you left behind in your home, Alice?"

"Well, I didn't bring my blow dryer or my straightener, and I certainly don't have my cell phone or my I-Touch. Is that what you mean?"

"You have left these things behind you—have you felt any hint of peace and joy out here in the midst of the wind and dust and heat?"

"Surprisingly, yes. And it has come at the oddest times. When we were pulling our handcarts up that steep hill, for example, I thought I had hit my limit. I have heard stories of people on treks such as this who have felt that angels were helping to push the carts when they themselves simply had no more energy. That was not the case with me. One of the 14-year-old boys in our family looked over at me just then and said, 'I'm glad that you came on this trek. I've been watching you, and you are a good person.' 'Thank you,' I replied. 'You're pretty awesome yourself.' And then we turned all our attention back to getting the cart's wheels over a couple of really big rocks. But that was enough to give me the courage to make it to the top. I knew I would be okay, and a certain peace crept into my tired legs and arms. I know that sounds kind of weird, because peace it supposed to be in your heart, but that's where I felt it."

"So you're telling me that you don't have any of the electronic devices that you have come to rely on so much every day, and yet somehow you found peace and happiness in the middle of one of the most difficult moments of your life. Why is that, Alice?"

"I know I sound like one of those corny 'feel good' radio ads, but I've been reminded that a nine-volt battery doesn't power the source of good feelings. It reminds me of when we were in Cambodia. We had just come from our comfortable home in the United States and couldn't figure out how some of these children and families who truly had nothing but the second-hand clothing they were wearing could be so happy. And when we came back home, so many of our friends seemed just miserable if they weren't spending more money in a week than some of those Cambodian families had to spend in a year. It just broke my heart, but I guess that sometimes I'm just like my spoiled friends. I mean, this is really hard. I miss my shower right now. And my bed. Oh, do I miss my bed!"

"Sure you do, Alice. And that's okay. Just don't confuse pleasure with happiness. That bed of yours provides great pleasure because of its comfort, but it doesn't provide lasting happiness. It's also okay to feel sadness, pain, and loneliness. But these emotions are not caused by the presence or absence of things, Alice. As you continue to learn what brings and detracts from happiness, you will learn what these pioneers have learned, and you will find that peace can be in your heart even when you are burying a newly died child in the snow because the ground is too frozen to dig a proper grave in."

"I remember on the flight home from Cambodia, I sat next

to Rick. On the other side of him was my dad. I remember them talking, and Rick said, 'These people have nothing, and yet they are happy.'"

"Alice, one of the greatest lessons that you can learn in this life is to understand the joy that comes from seeing all that life has to offer as a whole and then not succumb to the need to satisfy yourself in the moment.

"What else have you learned, Alice? I know you have been thinking of your great-grandmother and of a young woman named Emily Wall. What have they taught you?"

Alice's eyes grew a little misty. "I have learned that sometimes courage comes not so much from focusing on overcoming a particular challenge but rather from focusing on what lies beyond the challenge. After Emily's brother nearly drowned, the rest of the handcart company didn't believe that Emily could keep up with them. I felt very impressed once that she had the courage to do what she did not by making sure she could place one foot in front of the other thousands of times each day but rather by keeping in her mind an image of her entire family gathered together around the fireplace in a log home in the West. That image led her past the pain in her shoulders and the worry for her brother. Great-grandmother Rene did the same thing—she was so focused on the end result that she walked right through all the suffering along the way."

"Alice, you have discovered a secret that has eluded many brave men through the entire history of the world. People tend to focus on what stands in their way, not on where they are going. Courage to overcome obstacles is rooted in the vision of what is to be, not in overcoming what might go wrong. Never forget that, Alice. That is a lesson that will be worth more to you than any sum of money, for understanding the true nature of courage will allow you to accomplish anything you set your mind to.

"Now," and the old man's eyes just twinkled with mischief, "I think you'd best be catching up with the rest of your family. You still have a couple of miles to pull today, and I think they could really use your help!"

That evening, Alice pulled her trek journal out of her duffel bag in the handcart and wrote:

Life's lessons give me character. Bravery will allow me to succeed through any obstacles that I face.

I am honest, generous, patient, virtuous, kind, even keeled, perceptive, wise, and courageous.

Have an unyielding will, symbolize boldness and perseverance. Know in your heart that when you have committed and you are totally engaged, nothing can stop you.

Chapter 30

Alice could feel the "burn" start in her legs. It usually happened around the seven mile mark, and she had just past it about three minutes before. She had been in a self-imposed training since July1, preparing for the upcoming cancer walk-a-thon. She and Sue, her best friend, had been quite aggressive in signing up sponsors and they wanted to make sure that they were able to complete the course in the promised time and force every one who had signed up to pay up in support of a good cause.

But this morning Sue had been unable to meet her for their morning run, so Alice was on her own. Another half mile and she could stop.

She pushed hard that last half mile, pushing through the burn and the tired muscles and the desire to stop early. After all, who would know? Certainly not Sue. But no—she couldn't, wouldn't allow such thoughts in her head. And despite the pain and discomfort, she had to smile as she came in view of her personal finish line, for there, stretching like a yoga master and wearing a pair of well-worn gray sweats, was her guardian angel.

"Well done, Alice! A great finish, I must say. Doesn't it feel so good to push through to the end of a difficult task?"

"Why do I feel a teaching moment coming my way?" she managed to say between deep cleansing and refreshing breaths.

"Then I won't disappoint you, little one," he said, eyes twinkling in their familiar way. "We need today, more than ever before, people who are willing engage in their personal quest, people who will reach beyond limits, people who are prepared to live out their dreams and have the courage to do so.

"There are two things I would enjoy discussing with you this morning while I have you all to myself. First, often we see our goal or dream clearly in the distance, but the path to get there is murky and cloudy. We may envision something we want to do, find the motivation, gain the inspiration to start, and move along the path. But almost immediately we are presented with roadblocks of discouragement right in front of us.

"Such roadblocks can come anytime, but often they seem to show up just as we are nearing completion of our quest, but our vision is obscured to the point that we cannot see just where we are on the path, and don't realize how close to the end we are.

"Next, across the world I see people losing the ability to find joy in pursuit of their ambitions. Alice, if your heart is in whatever it is you want to do, you will do it! Passion brings the energy that delivers our desire. It builds a foundation that allows us to do even more as we begin to realize we have no limits.

"For just a moment, I want us to go to a place where your father overcame one of his greatest fears. But first let me give you some background.

"Your dad was born with acrophobia, or fear of heights."

"He was? I had no idea."

"Do you know he climbed to the top of the Grand Teton peak? It is 13,770 feet high and is the second highest peak in Wyoming. On that hike he could have failed had he just given up. Many have done so on that climb. We will join him there in just a minute.

"First you need a little background. As a young child, your dad was one day walking with your grandma up a staircase in a mall; the steps had open backs so you could see through to the ground floor. As they climbed up the staircase, at about 10–15 feet high, your dad fell to the nearest step, screaming at the top of his lungs in fear. Your grandma had no idea what was wrong or what may have hurt him. However, as soon as she bent over to help him, she learned that he was scared to death of the height, sensing he would fall. She actually had to carry him off those stairs.

"Now let's move forward to about ten years ago. He was climbing Angels Landing—I love that name—in Zion's Park. His group came to an area in the hike where the climbers needed to traverse a ridgeline about 18 inches across and 1,500 feet in the air. The Forest Service had placed a chain there for safety. Many were crossing at this point on the trail.

"In your dad's group were a variety of people in age and ability. As he approached the chain, he locked up in fear and couldn't move. His only choice was to turn around quickly to what he felt was safety and wait while others crossed. Friends tried to get him to change his mind, even offering to help, but nothing worked.

"While waiting, he noticed that many people with far less physical ability crossed with no hesitation at all. He knew he could walk a mile on the small end of a two-by-four without falling off—if it were on the ground. But this 18-inch ridge couldn't be negotiated, even with a chain to hold onto, because it was elevated.

"While waiting there that day for his hiking partners, he decided that it was time to realize his dream of crossing that narrow ridge to Angels Landing. He found in his heart the determination to overcome this phobia, knowing he had the skill set to succeed.

"On arriving home he contacted a friend who was a skilled mountain climber, asking him to teach your dad how to climb. Gladly this friend of your dad's took the challenge, knowing of his fears.

"On their first elementary climb, this friend could clearly see your dad's fear but enjoyed witnessing his determination. Their first climbs were short, but after time they had achieved a double-rope ascent. Before long, they agreed to climb to the summit of the Grand Teton.

"It was on this climb your dad portrayed his unyielding will. There is a place just after the saddle where hikers begin to see an area called 'Wall Street.' A rock ledge about 20 feet wide, gradually moves up the sheer cliffs of the mountain, closing down to just inches before a rock outcropping eliminates the foothold. Hikers at this point need to negotiate around the outcropping and are at least 1,500 feet off the ground. This is not a situation to be trifled with.

"Now hold my hand, Alice. The group with your dad is composed of twelve hikers who have all prepared for this hike. They are beginning to file into a resting area where they can begin to see Wall Street. They will stop here to prepare for the walk up to the outcropping. Your dad is about the eighth hiker to reach this spot. Notice that those who are already there are anxiously talking about what they see across the high mountain valley. We will be joining them in listening to their discussion now."

Alice focused her attention on the scene before her. "Hey, Jim, how are you holding up?" asked his friend. Those on the hike were all well aware of Jim's fear and knew why he was making this climb.

"Fine, I can't wait to summit! How are you all doing?"

On a rock about five feet away, Joe, the group's best mountaineer, was heavy in conversation with four other climbers. "Bob, I know that it looks challenging, but it really isn't that bad," Blaine remarked.

"Yes it is—we are all going to die!" Bob barked back.

Jim began to walk closer to see if he could help. Blaine saw him coming and pulled him to the side, "Jim, Bob is concerned, scared, and doesn't want to proceed."

"What? No way!"

"Even worse, he has started to psych out Joe as well, and you know that Joe is one of our best. Bob is truly frightened—I don't think he can continue on from here."

"Oh my gosh! Are you kidding me!" Alice could tell that her dad was waivering just a bit. Her guardian angel gently squeezed her hand and spoke confidently.

"Feel your dad's heart, Alice. It is beginning to beat really hard and fast, filling with the emotion of fear, which paralyzes him. He knows he will have a lockdown on his ability to proceed if his phobia is allowed time to dwell in his heart.

"Alice, feel and sense what happens next, for it will change your life. I want you to know exactly what your dad now experiences." Alice began to tremble uncontrollably as she had never felt fear before like she felt piercing her heart and mind now, yet she knew she had to go deeper. Her father's heart was seeking a way to persevere. "You're right, Alice. He is committed, and with this commitment he will find a way."

Alice noticed her dad wouldn't even look over at Wall Street to see what it was that had filled these men with fear. She could sense that he knew if he looked over, witnessing first hand what they were talking about, he too may give in. Recognizing that,

Jim walked far enough away from the group that he could no longer hear the details of their continued discussions. Once away, she watched as he bowed his head in silent prayer for several long minutes, then raise his eyes up to the heavens as if to acknowledge some specific instruction.

At that moment, the guardian angel closed off their vision of the climb, but he did not conclude his teaching. "Alice, four of the twelve hikers, including one of their best climbers, were so traumatized by the discussions that they chose to turn back with Bob. Although this was a challenging part of the climb, it was not the most difficult. Your dad went on to the summit, and after reaching his goal went back to Angels Landing and crossed there too."

"Thank you, Guardian Angel, for allowing me the experience of feeling what had only been a story in my youth. I learned something that I didn't think expect, too. May I share it with you?"

"Of course, Alice."

"When my dad first approached the small group who were frightened about going on, he was going to try to help them. But when he felt his own resolve weakening, he knew he had to get away from them in order to save any chance of reaching his own goals. Angel, I see that a lot with my friends. They want to help someone who is in some sort of danger, but they end up getting sucked into the problem too deeply, and then everyone gets hurt. My dad's actions taught me that sometimes we have to make sure we ourselves are safe before we can help another. It's not selfish to do that—it's just common sense. He had to maintain his focus in order to accomplish his goals and become what he supposed to become."

"That is very insightful, my young friend. Those who make a difference in our world live out their dreams. Your father was being true to himself when he stepped away from those who would dissuade him. Nothing can keep you from reaching the highest heights if you learn to stay the course, like your father did. Those who succeed do so by pushing through when others quit, sometimes when they are perhaps 99% of the way to success. If only they knew—they wouldn't and shouldn't give up. Alice, never give up on your dreams!

"Those who survive through the roadblocks, those who make a difference in our world, and those who are remembered—all these lived the impossible dream. We are living in a world today that is made up of the dreams of yesterday."

After Alice got home from her run, before she even took time to shower, she pulled out her journal and wrote:

Roadblocks will not stop me from reaching my dreams. I never give up, knowing that when I am committed nothing will stop me. I surround myself with dream makers.

I am honest, generous, patient, virtuous, kind, even keeled, perceptive, wise, courageous, and determined!

Chapter 31

Last night was one of the most amazing nights of my entire life.

A few months ago I was thinking of the many blessings that had come to our family because we had visited that beautiful country of Cambodia and remembered how RP's "guardian angels" had protected us one evening in a dark alleyway. All these years RP has tried to find his parents and his two younger sisters, and he has not succeeded. So I thought I would help do a kind of "reverse search." I made a handful of flyers using a picture of RP from Dad's high school yearbook and sent them to our friends in Cambodia, thinking that if RP couldn't find his family, maybe his family could stumble on RP.

Two weeks ago, a woman from a medical clinic in a remote mountainous village brought a child to the hospital where we had started our trip. The six-year-old daughter of a local leader was dying, and there was nothing to be done except help her to go as peacefully as possible. Somehow the village chief had heard of this hospital in Phnom Penh where children go to die, and he wanted his daughter to benefit from the hospital's services. A nurse brought the emaciated little girl in according to the father's wishes. She was so impressed with the paintings on the wall and with the spirit of the place.

Before the nurse left, she went in to see the doctor who ran the hospital to say thanks for her assistance, and as she did so, she noticed my flyer on the doctor's wall. Her face went white, then she became very excited. "Who is that boy?" she wanted to know.

"A friend of the American family who first brought happiness to this hospital five years ago when they painted the characters on the walls and reminded me why I was working here," was the reply. "Why do you ask?"

"That boy is my brother, whom I have not seen for many years," the nurse said. "How can I find him?"

That led to a very successful string of events that came to a conclusion yesterday evening, in our home, when we invited RP and his aunt over for dinner. Imagine their surprise when they came in the front door to find RP's two younger sisters and his aging parents waiting for them in our family room! I do not think that the tears stopped flowing all evening long. When RP left, taking his family with him, he gave each of us long and heartfelt hugs. I have never felt so much gratitude in a hug in my entire life! It just flowed like an electric current from him to me—wow!

As amazing as that was, however, that was not the biggest event of the evening, at least for me. After RP's family left and we cleaned up after dinner, we all went off to bed. I had just turned back the covers on my bed when I heard a familiar voice behind me. "Alice, that was a beautiful thing that you did." When I turned around, there was my guardian angel, wearing the same robe as always, smiling his usual smile, and looking right through me with the wisest eyes I've ever seen.

As nearly as I recall, this is what he said: "You need to know something about the day when I came to you in the temple. Wicked men were going to take your sisters but were diverted when they saw you—they knew you would be beautiful and were young enough that you could be more easily trained for their evil ways. When you strayed from your family, they saw their chance to take you and were close to doing so when my ability to manifest myself to you physically was granted. I came first to attend you just long enough to ensure your safety, but as I touched you I sensed immediately that you are very special.

"There wasn't time to accomplish anything other than to bless you and give you a gift that carried a spirit that you were familiar with. The bracelet was our physical connection while I sought permission to give you the eternal wisdom that accompanies the bracelet.

"For five years I patiently watched to make sure that you could handle the responsibilities of receiving and passing on the wisdom of the bracelet. At last I received permission to teach you. It has been an unforgettable and joyous experience for me.

"Those in my world realized how important your learning would be for you and for those whom you met in life. Many doors will be opened for you as you live out your life and share these life lessons in the right way. Guardian angels will be with you always as you help them bring good to mankind."

"Will I see you again?"

"Alice, you have been introduced to the magic of the bracelet. You don't need me anymore—your understanding will prove to be your greatest asset. Others over time will learn to follow that still, small voice in their heart and that it can be trusted. You follow that still, small voice, knowing what it is. Your knowledge will in turn build others' confidence and understanding.

"It is your duty now to lead the way."

"You avoided my question—will I see you again?"

"Alice, please know that whether you see me or not, I am here and will always be here. In fact, every person here on earth is surrounded by guardian angels who love them and will protect them—if they are allowed to do so. Here, close your eyes, little one." As I closed my eyes, I felt my angel place his right hand gently against my left cheek. "Now open your eyes, and tell me what you see."

As accustomed as I had become to my mentor's ways, I was unprepared for this. All about me were people! Real, living people, mortal people, each with differing opportunities and needs. And yes, surrounding the people were angels, each actively helping a mortal being. Some of the people felt alone and wondered whether they could push through their trials; it was around those that I saw the greatest number of supporting angels. No one was alone; everyone had the love and devotion of guardian angels. Each angel desperately wanted to share an eternal perspective with a loved one. They helped carry heavy loads, guided their mortals around threats, and gave simple hints to unanswered questions. I sensed that most angels were related to the mortals they were helping—some guardians had obviously lived in mortality, yet some were still waiting to come. This surprised me at first, but it somehow felt quite natural.

Not all of the guardian angels were from modern times. Some were in monk's robes, as my friend was, but others wore costumes from various ages and cultures of the world—Roman philosophers, Irish druids and priestesses, Italian priests, Chinese artists, South American farmers, African herders—men and women from all generations of time. The one constant was the light and love that seemed to emanate from each person's face, especially around the eyes.

"Alice, guardian angels have always been and will always surround you and everyone else in times of need and in those times when trouble-free directions may simply improve life. Yes, they have assignments, yet they also help each other out in fulfilling common

goals. On a personal note, they care for you. They understand how important you are in getting the word out regarding their true nature, even their existence. Believe me, you will never be alone, and neither will anyone else, particularly in time of need."

At this point, the wise old angel reached out with his left hand and held my face lovingly cupped between his ancient hands. "I know that you have asked specifically whether we will see each other again. Little one, it wouldn't be fair for me to answer your question—your life is better lived not fully understanding what lies ahead. You must always keep a journal, however.

"Your family, friends, and others around you will gain from your experiences and interactions with them, but countless more lives will be touched by your sharing your story. The world one day will read of your life's adventures through publication of your chronicle. I can't wait to see the lives you touch—it will astound you!"

I committed to my guardian angel to write my feelings and experiences so I can share them with all who will read or listen. And then he was gone, leaving behind a bracelet, an ancient blessing, and a promise of good things to come.